THE HAND THAT PULLS YOU UNDER

JAMES FLYNN

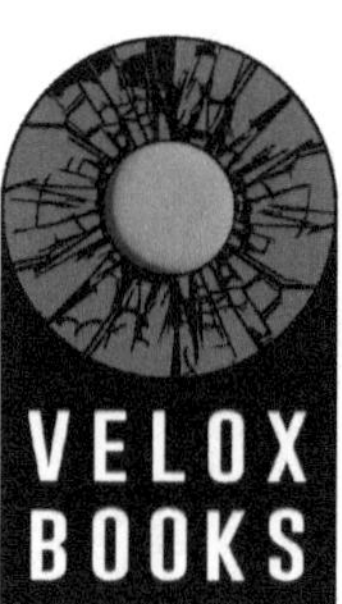

Published by arrangement with the author.

Copyright © 2025 by James Flynn.

All rights reserved.

YOU'RE READING ANOTHER TERRIFYING COLLECTION FROM

**FOLLOW VELOX TO KEEP
THE NIGHTMARES COMING:**

For the universe, in all its absurdity

CONTENTS

THE RESIDENTS OF HILLTOP HARROWS

An old abandoned building
High up upon the hill
The stuff of myth and legend
The rumours so unreal

Its residents were crazy
Or that's what people said
At night they drank and partied
Intoxicated heads

If weird is what you're into
They have it by the barrel
The enigmatic folks
Of loony Hilltop Harrows

B rian didn't exist. Sure, he existed in the physical sense, but in the hearts and minds of all who used to know him he was little more than a faint memory.

He'd been a drifter for many years now, sleeping in a different place every night, getting by on the ever-decreasing savings he'd stashed away during his former working days. Cheap hotels and B&Bs were his home, especially the dirty, rundown ones, the kind that had peeling wallpaper, no clothes hangers in the wardrobes, no toiletries in the bathroom, and tacky paintings on the walls in ugly-looking frames.

Things hadn't always been this way; there'd been a time when Brian had been "normal" like everyone else. Normal in the sense that he'd had a decent education, a steady job, a steady income, a good car, a nice-looking girlfriend, a house with a mowed lawn out the front to impress the neighbours, that kind of thing. But his mini empire had come crashing down like a house of cards a few years back after the police pulled him over on his way to work. He'd been hungover from a party the night before, alcohol lingering on his breath in a pungent smell, and his licence got taken away for six months.

A domino effect ensued.

After being late for work a handful of times his boss grew impatient and fired him, after missing several rent payments his landlord grew disgruntled and evicted him, and after losing the house his pretty young girlfriend scarpered quicker than a hare with its tail on fire. The unfortunate affair rendered him distraught for a while, yes, but he'd still had some secret savings. Slipping into an unusual kind of nomadic lifestyle, he began roaming the streets and districts of Mapharno City like a leisurely lost soul.

And in all honesty, he quite liked his stress-free life. He enjoyed a kind of permanent holiday, rising at ten a.m. in some dank motel for breakfast, wandering through parks and town centres during midday to people watch and read newspapers, and, providing he'd stuck to his strict daily budget, he'd then enjoy a hot meal in some low-end restaurant before finding another flea pit to spend the night in. It suited him just fine, but he now had a problem. His savings were running low, *dangerously* low, and when he opened his eyes to another mouldy hotel ceiling one Tuesday morning, his wallet almost empty on the bedside table next to him, he knew that he'd have to downgrade to a park bench or a motorway underpass sometime very soon if he wanted to continue eating hot meals.

An underpass seemed cosier than a park bench. It was rough at first, of course, but after a fortnight or so the cardboard boxes felt more like thin blankets, and the cold night air in the early hours lost some of its bite due to the sweaters and shirts he'd accumulated from washing lines. The underpass wasn't quite as lush as a two-star hotel room, of course, but like all things in life he got used to it after a while.

He also made some new friends.

Brian had neighbours under the motorway flyover, people who slept a few feet away from him on either side in their own boxes and torn clothing. Most were men, young and old, but a couple of eccentric bag ladies were resident there too. In the afternoon they'd all gather around a fire and tell stories, drinking cider from paper cups and smoking rollups with tobacco taken from discarded cigarette butts. And it was on one of these blissful afternoons that Brian first learnt about Hilltop Harrows.

'What's that?' he asked, when one of his crusty comrades mentioned it for the first time.

'Hilltop Harrows is an old factory on the hill in District 10,' spat his grimy friend, puffing a rollup through the yellowed hairs of his beard. 'It's home to a large squatting community. They've been there for years.'

Brian didn't really think much about this factory after hearing about it for the first time, but the more he socialized with members of the underground homeless community the more the name kept popping up. Conversing with various oddballs and outcasts during his daily wanderings, descriptions of this decrepit factory were never too far away. Tales of wild parties, homemade liquor, drugs, and curious oddities within the walls of this old building persisted and eventually sparked a strong curiosity within him, and he began to ask people for more details about this seemingly legendary place.

And it was for this reason, when the time came to move on from the underpass in search of a new home, that Brian's next port of call was Hilltop Harrows.

Hilltop Harrows sat atop a long hill like some kind of rectilinear mutated growth. Networks of pipes and gulleys snaked their way across the crumbling architecture, and black windows stared out from its rotting brickwork like the eyes of a demented soul. Looking up at its exterior as he climbed the grassy slope towards it, Brian tried to guess what the old place had been used for when it was still functional.

Reaching the entrance of the building, he felt his nerves kick in. Was he really just going to walk into this place and make it his home? Would the occupants of this giant squat simply accept him with open arms? The stories he'd heard about them conjured up images of an outlandish cult, a crazed clan, so was it really wise to just stroll in there alone, bold as brass, and simply hope that they were welcoming and hospitable?

Probably not, he thought, as he lingered a few metres away from the factory's façade, but what did he have to lose? The thought of returning to the underpass didn't appeal to him, a park bench even less so, and with his bank balance down to single digits he didn't really have much else.

After taking a deep breath and running a hand through his greasy, matted hair, he pushed open one of the big entrance doors and walked in.

A large, wide room confronted him, possibly an old production line, with dusty machinery dotted about the place like ancient relics. A dry chemical smell tinged the air, and the orange afternoon light from outside painted everything in hazy tones.

Evidence of residency was everywhere: empty beer bottles on the floor, crushed takeaway boxes under desktops, blackened cigarette butts on the flat corners of machines, dried-up condoms on windowsills and graffiti scrawled across flaky walls. There was also a shiny, well-trodden pathway along one side of the room, a trail leading to another section of the building, and Brian tentatively followed it.

It was then that he met one of the occupants of Hilltop Harrows for the first time.

A voice rose up from a shadowy corner somewhere, throwing him completely off guard: 'The length of your nose is 5.6 centimetres, the circumference of your head is 57.2 centimetres, and the tip of your right shoe stands 3.7 metres away from the tip of my right shoe.'

The voice echoed through the acrid air like a detached recording, a random sequence of measurements emanating from a mechanical tongue. Then, in the manner of a statue coming to life, a lean man stepped forward from the gloom. He had a long face and a neat moustache, he was dressed in a formal navy blue blazer, and he carried an air of class and nobility that put Brian on a defensive back foot. Without altering his rigid expression one iota, the regal-looking man continued his pedantic dialogue with a sense of entitlement: 'Your pupils have a surface area of 3.4 square millimetres, your irises have a surface area of 24.1 square millimetres, the radius of the middle finger on your left hand—'

Brian could take no more than a few seconds of this crazed dialogue. 'I'm sorry, what... Who are you?'

The man halted in his speech, stunned, perhaps a little offended, then said, 'My name is Alan. Two syllables, four letters. First, twelfth, first, and fourteenth letters of the alphabet. One-sixth of an inch high if typed using twelve-point font on a word processor, one-seventy-second of an inch high if typed using one-point font.'

Brian spurted out a half-coherent reply, dizzy with confusion and befuddlement. Studying Alan in the dim light, he could see that there was something odd about his eyes, an unnatural glint. Before he could ascertain what it was, though, another voice rose up from somewhere behind him.

'Hello, fella! I'm Gavin. I've never seen you here before. How ya doin'? All right? Are ya lost or something? I suppose ya must be, wandering in here like this. Mind you, ya might not be. How the hell should I know? I haven't got a clue. You could own the bloody place for all I know! I hope ya don't, mind you, because then we'd all be in trouble. Although maybe it'd be good in some ways. Don't ask me to name them, mind you, because I couldn't. And even if I could, I wouldn't. D'ya know what I mean? I don't suppose ya do, actually. Why would ya? I'm harping on again like a lunatic, aren't I? Harping on. Where did the word "harping" come from? Have ya ever played a harp? One of those big things? It's like a classical instrument. A friend of mine had one once, and he let me have a go on it. Beautiful thing, it was. Shame the notes I played weren't very beautiful, mind you. It sounded like a cat being strangled. Not that I'm familiar with the sound a cat makes when it gets strangled, I'll have you know. I'm an animal lover, me. I used to be a vegetarian. I was vegetarian for about eight years until I accidentally ate meat one night whilst pissed. When I realised what I'd done the next day, I thought, "Well, I quite fancy a bacon sandwich now." And that was it. Meat eater again! I don't really eat bacon sandwiches anymore, though, strangely enough. I can't remember the last time I had one. It's funny how your taste buds change, isn't it? We change over time. It's like we become different people. Do we actually become different people, though? Or do we... Cor! Listen to us! We're straying into the realm of philosophy now! Bit deep, eh? Mind you, I kind of see myself as an amateur philosopher in a way. Come to think of it, I suppose we all are. We're born philosophers, thinking about this and that all day, pondering about the many nuances of life and existence. That reminds me of a song. "Think all day, work and play." Is that it? Is that how it goes? Or is it "Everyday, I work and play"? No, no, I've got it now, it's...'

Brian stood there for several minutes as a small, gentle-looking man with short hair reeled off this continuous thought stream, throwing word after word at him like bullets from a Gatling gun. Eventually, when it became clear that he simply wasn't going to stop, Brian smiled as politely as he could and peeled himself away from him, walking on through the innards of the derelict factory in an exploratory manner.

Each section of the building brought new surprises. There were a considerable number of squatters living there, and each one reacted to his presence in a slightly different way. Some remained seated in the shadows, leaning against the hard walls in an alcohol or Valium daze, others approached him with childlike curiosity. There was no visible hierarchy, nobody seemed to be in charge, and so eventually he relaxed a little bit and started to look for a place to lie down.

A long line of sleeping bags and pillows were laid out along the edge of a second warehouse floor, some empty some full, and so he traipsed over in that direction and unpacked his own from his rucksack. Despite the incessant background noise of chatter and murmuring, coupled with his slight unease about being inside the notorious Hilltop Harrows building, Brian dozed off within a few minutes of climbing into his tattered sleeping bag. He had no idea what Hilltop Harrows was really all about, he had no idea who these weird people really were, but he was far too tired to work any of it out.

He would return to these questions tomorrow.

The factory looked different in the morning light, more spacious perhaps, and Brian pulled himself up from his pillow to take it all in. Strangers snored and slumbered either side of him, huddled in their stinking pits, and semi-naked forms wandered around near the dusty machinery like confused employees of a time gone by.

Rubbing the sleep from his eyes, he noticed a familiar face peering over at him from the other side of the room, flanked by two others. Alan, the measuring man, sat across from him with two women, and all three of them gazed at him with benevolent smiles.

Alan still wore his smart blazer, his hair neatly parted and immaculately combed, but the wild look in his eyes seemed to have gone. The woman seated to his right was large, plump, and had a motherly look about her. She wore thick glasses and her dark hair was bobbed near the shoulders. The woman on the other side of him was older, much older, and wore a brimmed hat with a veil which covered her eyes.

'Sleep well?' Alan said in his well-spoken tone.

'Erm, yes. Thanks. I hope you don't mind—'

'We don't mind you being here at all,' said the plump woman, cutting in. 'I hope Alan didn't scare you last night, by the way.'

'Not at all,' Brian said, lying. 'I, err...I thought I'd stop by because I needed a place to stay.'

'The more the merrier, sweetheart. I'm Susan, by the way.'

'Nice to meet you. I'm Brian.'

'Are you hungry?'

Brian was famished.

They were sat around a table—a stack of wooden pallets piled on top of each other—eating fox meat that Susan had just finished cooking on an oil drum barbeque. Alan seemed a lot more grounded now, more level-headed, and he didn't indulge in any of the mathematical observations of the previous evening. Over the course of breakfast Brian learned that Alan was an ex-accountant, a career man back in the day, a middle-class citizen who'd stumbled upon hard times. He'd been living at Hilltop Harrows for sixteen years, but still clung to his civilized roots as much as he could. Susan was an ex-housewife who'd lost her husband and two children in a car accident, sleeping on friends' sofas for a few months until she eventually ended up on the streets. Her story was tragic, and she told it with pain lacing her voice. By the time she finished, Brian felt almost privileged in comparison.

The old lady with the veil was harder to work out. She remained silent the whole time they sat there, quietly chewing strips of crispy meat, the top half of her countenance concealed by the thin black veil. She responded to the name Doreen now and again with minute tilts of her head, but apart from that her communication was extremely limited.

'You'll be safe enough here,' said Alan, with a wink. 'We get a few dodgy people here now and then, but they usually don't stay for long. And as for the authorities: I think they've forgotten about this place.'

'Why don't you show him the view, Alan?' suggested Susan, giving him a nudge.

'Yes, good idea.' Alan nodded, scratching his moustache. 'There's quite a sight to be seen up on the rooftop. Come on, I'll take you up there.'

Brian got up and followed Alan towards a dim staircase. He wanted to ask him why he'd behaved so strangely the night before, why he seemed to have a split personality, but somehow he couldn't quite do it. There was an aspect of Alan's demeanour that prevented him from doing so, his lordly body language and proud mannerisms making it too hard. He restrained himself from asking the question for now, deciding instead to wait for the right moment.

They made their way up the four floors of the building, climbing the manky concrete steps. They didn't stop, but Brian was able to catch a brief glimpse of each level as they passed them. The first floor had a handful of vacated offices, with sleeping figures visible through open doorframes; the second floor had a vandalized laboratory with a couple of stray dogs running around the place; the third floor had a conference room with a large circular table, with the remnants of what looked suspiciously like a sex party on top of it; and the fourth floor consisted solely of a single corridor with a few rooms on either side of it. A faint, ghostly light emanated from under the far door at the end, but Alan ushered him on before he could make anything out.

A steel ladder led up to the rooftop, and they both climbed it.

From the top of the factory, the sprawling metropolis of Mapharno City could be seen on the horizon. High rises and apartment complexes sat in the morning haze like filaments rising from the Earth, rooftops and chimneys forming a jagged line from left to right.

'Beautiful,' said Brian. 'What a view.'

'Indeed,' replied Alan, turning his grey head to scan the vista. 'I usually come up here in the afternoon. I never tire of it.'

The view seemed to mellow Alan somehow, lowering his fortified manner, and Brian saw his chance to ask the question. 'Alan,' he said, gently, 'do you remember anything of last night?'

Still looking out towards the distance, Alan murmured, 'I remember.'

'Why were you—'

Alan's jaw tightened for the briefest moment, then he said, with strain in his voice, 'Some of us eat from the garden, Brian. Some of us don't. It's a personal choice. For me, well...after you've lived here for a while, I suppose you become a part of the place.'

'Eat from the garden?'

'You'll see.' Alan sighed. 'But take my advice: think carefully before you dabble in the fruit of the garden, because you're never truly the same again.'

Brian didn't push the topic any further, but Alan's cryptic comments stayed in his mind for the duration of time that he was up on the roof. And after he descended back down into the gloomy guts of the factory, he decided to make it his mission to find out where this mysterious garden was.

As the days and weeks wore on, Brian felt more and more at home at Hilltop Harrows. The place was wild, strange and unpredictable, but that was part of its charm. People came and went, vagrant types, travellers, yobs, drifters, but a core community always remained. Alan, Susan, Gavin, and Doreen were among this core community, but there were others too. Certain groups of people occupied the upper floors on a permanent basis, mostly hippyish types and societal misfits, and there was also a community of young women who'd claimed the third floor as their own and converted it into a kind of feminine parlour.

It didn't take too long for him to solve the mystery of the aforementioned garden. In fact, it turned out to be more of a metaphor. The name was a reference for a variety of mouldy crevices and corners within the building, where mushrooms and fungus was known to sprout from. This fungus was treated as a valuable delicacy among select members of the community, and about once every three or four weeks there'd be an organised Harvest Night. On Harvest Nights a designated person would walk around the damp, filthy crevices of the factory where the mushrooms grew in abundance, pulling up the stalks and collecting them all in an old takeaway box.

It was on these nights that things got interesting.

The mushrooms were consumed in excess, especially by the permanent members of the squatting community. Alan, the smartly dressed gentleman, would chomp four or five of them down with his dinner on Harvest Nights, transforming himself into his measuring man alter ego. Susan would often eat one or two with a cup of warm cider, altering her personality in ways which were harder to describe. She became more alert somehow, more organised, swallowed up by an OCD-like desire to keep everything neat, tidy, and orderly. If anyone asked her the time during a Harvest Night she'd be able to tell them without looking at a watch, right down to the second, and her podgy hands would constantly be picking things up and moving things, arranging them in neat lines or rows. Gavin, aka The Chatty Man, had a particularly strong appetite for the factory fungus, and he'd unashamedly munch six or seven of the purple-headed mushrooms every single time he got the chance. The shrooms had an obvious effect on Gavin, turning him into a walking word generator, spewing out rapid sentences for hours on end.

But, without a doubt, the most intriguing person to observe on Harvest Nights was Doreen. The mushrooms had such a strong effect on her that she could only eat one under close supervision, and even then it was often too overwhelming for her. Whilst intoxicated by the purple-headed mushrooms, her old brain swimming with psilocybin, she would inexplicably begin to vomit over her own lap in violent bursts and sprays. For a long time, Brian was oblivious as to the cause of this sickness, until one night someone informed him that the mushrooms gave her the ability to taste colours. The old lady had been an artist in her heyday, selling hundreds of paintings, and the factory fungus tapped into her innate affinity for colour and hue. With the hallucinogen swimming around her system, the flickering candles and the bulky machinery and the dancing figures on the factory floor would overload her visual senses, causing her to chunder all over herself like an overindulgent child on a candy binge.

Nobody knew how the mushrooms were going to affect them until they tried them. A new squatter might arrive at the factory and randomly try some for fun, then completely lose their sense of passing time. A simple question would be thrown their way, a small inquiry like, "Do you have a cigarette?", and after an hour or two, later on during the night, they would suddenly pipe up and mumble their response as though the question had just been asked. Other people would submerge completely into their own heads, having conversations for eight hours with figures from their memories, people from the past, oblivious to the goings on right in front of their faces.

After observing the effects of this fungus on many occasions, sitting in on these Harvest Night parties, Brian began to suspect that it tinkered with the inherent traits of the users, intensifying some quality within them and magnifying it to comical proportions. Alan, for example, used to be an accountant during his working years, with a proclivity towards numbers and figures, and so the shrooms turned him into a flesh-and-blood calculator. Gavin, it was learned, used to work as a radio presenter on a pirate station before arriving at Hilltop Harrows, and so the mushrooms amplified his talkative nature. Doreen's visual, artistic talents were played upon, ramping them up to ridiculous levels, and Susan's motherly, organizational tendencies were heightened and exaggerated whenever she indulged in the fruit of the garden.

Another interesting example could be seen on the third floor.

The women in the parlour, who worked occasionally in the red-light districts of the city, enjoyed Harvest Nights in unprecedented style. An entire batch of mushrooms would be reserved for their quarters alone, strictly for them and their lucky guests, fueling the unstoppable paroxysm of lust, passion, and frenzy that would inevitably erupt.

Brian could never forget the first time he walked in on one of these steamy evenings by accident. He'd been talking to Gavin—or, to be more accurate, he'd been *listening* to Gavin as he spewed his usual stream of nonstop verbosity at him—taking a social stroll around the factory to stretch his legs as he sometimes did on Harvest Nights, when he inadvertently wandered into the girls' dwelling during a moment of disorientation. The sight that confronted him caused him to stop in the doorway like a stunned schoolboy gazing up at a shelf of pornographic magazines in a local newsagent.

There'd been asses and torsos everywhere, maniacal thrusting hips and screaming mouths in every corner of the candlelit floor. Legs pointed towards ceilings, varnished fingernails clawed sweat-covered backs, lips twisted in frantic desire, sandwiched bodies bounced back and forth amidst a cacophony of slapping and squelching noises, swollen members stabbed and swayed like meaty swords, and this riot of heated gymnastics was punctuated further still by an assortment of twisted facial expressions, staring out of the orgasmic haze like gurning hallucinating nymphs. The spectacle had been exhausting for Brian just to watch, especially with Gavin providing a rapid detailed commentary in his ear, but it'd been a sight to behold, and one that he would never forget.

The nature and origin of the mushrooms were a mystery. They were clearly a special variant of some kind, or maybe a mutation, but Brian was oblivious as to what gave them their special power. The thought crossed his mind on more than one occasion that a chemical residue left over from the factory's operational days might've held a clue. Could a medicinal residue be merging with the fungus, he wondered, augmenting the psilocybin to create a truly brain-altering psychedelic? This mystery nagged away at him more and more as he observed people during Harvest Nights, and on top of this there was also the mystery of the fourth floor.

There was little authority in Hilltop Harrows, no boss or leader, but at the same time there seemed to be an unspoken rule amongst the residents that the fourth floor was out of bounds to all but a select few. And this rule was never broken. Even on Harvest

Nights, when Alan was informing people of the thickness of their eyelashes and the size of the factory floor in square inches, when Gavin was retelling a conversation he'd heard on a documentary fifteen years ago, when the prostitutes were enjoying multiple climaxes up on the third floor, and when the old lady was vomiting profusely into her lap due to an overloading of sensory colours, even then, at the apex of the insanity, the mood would turn sour and edgy if anyone was spotted venturing up towards the fourth floor.

As time went on, however, it became impossible for Brian to resist the urge to visit the fourth floor. He simply had to know what was up there, and it became the main focus of his time and attention. He started to monitor everyone's habitual movements in order to work out the best time to do it, diligently making mental notes on the squatter's tendencies and routines. In the morning numerous residents would head into the city to beg and shoplift, but Susan and the old lady were always around somewhere, tidying up or preparing scraps of food. In the early afternoon the prostitutes would rise from their slumbers and head out in their tiny skirts and high heels to make some cash, but then Alan would often be up on the rooftop at this time, within ear's reach of where he wanted to go.

As unlikely as it seemed, late evening provided the most ideal time to sneak up to the fourth floor without being seen. The girls would still be out working the streets, Alan would be down from the roof, and most of the others would be smoking, drinking, and popping Valiums downstairs on the factory floor. Brian waited patiently for the right evening—which he decided was just before the next Harvest Night was due, in order to avoid any unpredictable behavior—and then slipped upstairs on the pretense of retrieving an item of clothing from the first floor offices.

There were one or two people lounging around the offices smoking bongs and pipes, but nobody really took any notice of him as he ascended the stairs. He reached the fourth floor easily and then gazed down the silent corridor before him with trepidation. Three wooden doors were visible on each side, some busted and hanging from their hinges, the vacant shells of the managerial offices visible through the cracks and gaps. Out of instinct he headed for the door furthest away, the door he'd seen light coming out of when Alan had taken him up to see the rooftop view. He edged towards it like a tip-toeing cat, noticing the faint light spilling out from under its bottom lip once again.

Placing his shaky palm over the door handle, he pulled it down and entered.

The room had an orange glow from the setting sun outside, a set of open blinds on the far wall letting it all seep in. Looking around, Brian could see thousands of scribblings and markings all over the place, numbers, words, drawings, and geometric shapes all drawn across the plasterboard walls in what appeared to be crayon and marker pen. For a long time, he was so engrossed and distracted by these elaborate markings, so absorbed in the visual onslaught of etchings all around him, that he failed to notice that he wasn't alone in the room. A seated figure was down on the ground before him, a small silhouette by his feet. It was a boy, no older than nine or ten, and he stared up at Brian from a makeshift nest of cushions and pillows. The sight of the child damn near took Brian's breath away, such was the intensity of his presence. His young round face held a knowing look that shouldn't have been there, the smooth contours of his countenance revealing an inner wisdom way beyond his tender age, a wisdom that should've belonged to a more seasoned soul.

For what seemed like an eternity, nothing happened. Not physically, anyway. Brian was off somewhere, a million miles away, lost in the labyrinth maze of the boy's irises. He was walking through mists of time, swimming through the spinning nuclei of atoms, wading through tides of consciousness. It was as though the boy's eyes contained everything he ever wanted to know, everything he ever yearned to discover, and they pulled his entire focus towards them like glistening magic boxes. He would've stayed this way for an endless length of time, held in the child's hypnotic stare, if it hadn't been for the voice rising up behind him.

'He was born here, you know. Here, in this very room.'

Brian broke out of his daze, turning on his heel. Susan stood in the doorway just behind him, grinning, her hands resting on her wide hips. 'He's... He's your son?' he stuttered.

'Yes.' She nodded. 'Interesting chap, isn't he?'

Brian tried to control his nausea, but the situation was overwhelming. Everything was suddenly weighing down upon him like a thousand invisible hands: the drawings and equations swirling in his peripheral vision, the boy's stare penetrating the back of his head, and Susan's demanding expression right in front of him.

'What... What's wrong with him?' was all he could think to say.

'Wrong?' frowned Susan. 'I wouldn't put it like that. There's nothing wrong with my Harvey. In fact, he's...' Susan's words became inaudible to Brian as everything inexplicably fell into place. That name, *Harvey*, was the only clue that he needed.

'The... The mushrooms...' he muttered.

'They're somehow responsible for his condition, yes,' replied Susan, candidly. 'His father took them regularly, as do I. I suppose it was inevitable that he was conceived on a Harvest Night. You could say that they're in his blood.'

'What... What does he see? What does he...do?'

'We're not quite sure,' Susan said, casting a loving smile down towards the boy. 'Nobody's ever heard him speak.'

Brian turned back around and faced the room. It was crushing and claustrophobic now, the endless markings all around him resembling the tendrils of a nervous system or the circuitry of a space station. The boy was a silent spider sitting in the middle of its web of information, a bird tucked into its intricate nest of data. Watching the youngster as he sat there stationary in an almost inhuman pose, Brian realized that there were other levels of consciousness apart from the standard human experience. In the same way that a bat or a cockroach experiences the world in a radically different way to a *Homo sapiens*, Brian got the feeling that the boy was watching him through a unique lens of his own, sensing things and observing things that only he could fathom.

'See that over there?' Susan said, pointing towards some writing that'd been scrawled along a skirting board in blue crayon. 'That's a conversation me and Alan had a few days before he was born.'

Brian squinted down at the lines of handwriting. 'What? You mean he—'

'He remembered it, word for word. At first I had no idea what it was, but when Alan saw it he remembered that it was a conversation we had while I was pregnant.' She smiled again at the boy. 'You were listening, weren't you honey?'

'That... That's incredible,' whimpered Brian. 'And... And what about this over here?' he said, pointing to another set of scrawls by the shuttered window.

'Ah, now that's a special one. Me and Doreen spent weeks trying to work that one out. We read it over and over but couldn't get it. He was only six years old when he wrote that, too.'

'But what is it?'

'It's a section of dialogue from a novel I once read.'

'When you were pregnant with him? You mean...he heard you reading it?'

Susan shook her head. 'No. I read that book about fifteen years ago. Way before I even met his father. I asked one of the girls downstairs to type it into Google for me, using her phone, and the search results sprang up a page for a book. As soon as I saw it, I remembered that I'd read it.'

Brian was shaking. This couldn't be real; it just couldn't be. If what Susan was saying was true, the boy had somehow retained and recorded a memory of a conversation he'd heard when he was merely a fetus, as well as inheriting a memory from his mother which had been created before he was even conceived.

The boy still hadn't moved since Brian entered the room, his stubby limbs as stiff as a rag doll's. The infantile eyes continued to watch on with an unblinking stare that permeated Brian's skin, rattled his core, and made him feel as though he were under some immense spotlight. The boy was life intensified, consciousness plus, existence magnified. To feel his gaze upon you was to feel the gaze of a vast crowd all at once, the attention of a large audience, the focus of an entire species.

'I need to get some air,' Brian croaked, feeling his legs growing weak. He made for the door but then stopped after a couple of paces. A series of pictures caught his eye halfway up one of the walls, organic shapes that'd been out of his line of sight. Under normal circumstances they could've been passed off as innocent, childish doodles, hardly worthy of a second look, but this was anything but a normal circumstance. 'Susan, have you...have you ever read any books on evolution?'

She gave him an odd look. 'No. Why?'

'Have you ever given him any science books? Dinosaur picture books or anything?'

'No. What are you on about?'

Brian looked at the drawings again, then said, 'Has he ever left this room?'

'For your information, no,' replied Susan, a touch defensively. 'I once tried to take him downstairs, but the experience was too overwhelming for him. By the time we reached the end of the corridor he was drooling at the mouth from sensory overload. But what are you getting at, anyway?'

'Susan, there are drawings over here of prehistoric animals. Early marine creatures, reptiles, bipedal hominids. How—'

'He must've reproduced something I once saw.' Susan shrugged. 'Maybe they're images from a show I watched on TV once.'

'Yes, maybe,' mumbled Brian. 'Or...'

'Or what?'

'Or maybe he can see history. Maybe he can see the history that's carried within our genes and our DNA.'

'History in our genes and DNA?' She scoffed, looking him up and down. 'When did you become a scientist?'

'I'm not, it's just... Oh, it doesn't matter.'

Back in the day, back when he'd led a normal life, Brian used to read a few books here and there. Science books, occasionally. And right now, looking over at these scribblings on the wall, he was seeing representations of trilobites, long-beaked birds, ancient primates, and a swirly pattern that looked suspiciously like the DNA double helix. He was seriously close to collapsing now, the atmosphere in the small room stuffy and suffocating, but he had to ask one more question before peeling himself away.

'Susan, what do you know about the company who used to own this building?'

'About the what?'

'The company who used to own this building. Who were they? What were they?'

'Oh, I don't know. They might've made tablets and medicine, but I'm not sure. Why? What's gotten into you?'

Brian squinted through the dim orange light towards the boy's dangerously alert face. What did it feel like to be inside that head? he wondered. What did it feel like to see the world through those eyes? The boy was a product of the infamous purple mushroom, a creation of the Harvest Night hallucinogen, possibly even a byproduct of a dubious pharmaceuticals company—was his existence a blissful dream or a ghastly nightmare?

'Brian, answer me!' cried Susan, nudging him.

'Huh? Err, nothing. Nothing's gotten into me. Don't worry, I...I just need some air.'

Unable to take anymore, Brian staggered out into the corridor and ran for the stairs, trying desperately to keep hold of his wits and his sanity.

The sky outside the tall factory windows was murky and dark, and another wild Harvest Night was in full swing. A healthy batch of fungus had been collected from the mouldy corners of the premises, and there was more than enough for everyone to get their fix. And this time around, on this particular night in question, Brian was indulging with the others.

Or at least, everybody thought he was.

When the takeaway box full of shrooms had been passed around, he'd put his hand in and grabbed a generous heap for himself, much to the surprise of those around him.

'Be careful,' Alan had said, counting the white stalks in Brian's palm. 'And be sure.'

Brian had nodded, thanked him for his concern, then proceeded to make a fake show of placing them into his mouth and consuming them. As far as everyone else was concerned, he'd swallowed them all. But in actual fact, they'd all been stuffed into his pocket for a different purpose. This act of deceit had taken place over an hour ago now, and the real consumers, the ones with the factory fungus actually circulating through their systems, were beginning to show signs of *coming up*.

Gavin, for one, was on good form, following Brian around the factory floor with his endless spiel: 'I can't believe you've eaten them, Brian. I didn't think you'd ever do it. Ya look as though you're coming up on them now, actually. Do ya feel anything? I bloody do! Things are starting to dance and sway. Look at that machine over there. Ya see that? Is it a machine? I've seen it a million times, but it looks different now. Ya see? This is what they do to ya. They distort ya perception, they distort ya time, they distort everything! Can ya feel anything yet? I definitely can now. Colours. Colours and thoughts. It's like they make ya feel at one with nature or something. Did I ever tell ya about the time I did magic mushrooms on a camping trip back in the day? We were camped out on a field somewhere. It might've just been a local park, come to think of it! That's the kind of thing we did back then. Anyway, someone spilt some beer on their sleeping bag. Or at least they thought they did. They were so out of their head they couldn't be sure. But they needed to find out, ya see, so they pulled their sleeping bag out of their tent and got everyone to feel it to see if it was wet or dry. There were six of us if I remember rightly, all crowded around feeling this sleeping bag to see if it was wet or dry. But do ya think we could decide? Could we bollocks! We were all so out of it we didn't know whether we were touching a wet sleeping bag or a dry sleeping bag! It's the shrooms, I tell ya! They mess with ya! But these ones are different, though, Brian. Be careful, honestly. Have ya ever done them before? Normal ones, I mean? Whoa! What was that? I'm seeing things now! Are ya seeing things yet? Ya look a bit tripping. You're gonna love it, I tell ya! Hopefully ya will. You can go on a bad one, mind you, if you're not careful. Some people scare themselves by thinking negatively. They think about spiders or bugs or something. Or they just imagine that people are watching them or talking about them or something. Don't you get like that, will ya? Whoa! Look at that wall! What colour is that? Is it grey or blue? I've seen that wall a million times, but it's never looked like that before. It's changing colour! Can ya see that? It's actually changing colour! It's a chameleon. A chameleonic wall. Is that a real word? *Chameleonic*? Well, if it's not, it should be! Maybe I should claim it? Can you claim words like that? Can you claim words at the patent office? It'd be bloody good if you could. That way, every time somebody said the word *chameleonic* they'd have to pay me money! Mind you, come to think of it, I doubt many people would use the word very often. I'd be better off patenting a word like *the*. How many times do people use the word *the* on an average day? I'd be rich within about ten minutes! It'd be hard to enforce, though, I imagine. I mean, how could you keep track of everyone using your word? You'd have to install microphones all over the place. Microphones in the street, microphones in coffee shops, microphones in...'

And so on and so forth.

With a couple of diversionary tactics Brian managed to escape the barrage of words and gibberish, biding his time to execute his plan.

Doreen was over in the corner, her eyes—just visible through the thin veil—darting left and right like pinballs, with wet pools of vomit staining the front of her floral dress. Susan was busy arranging things in front of her, lining up pieces of cutlery and beads on the floor so that they sat in neat, orderly lines. Sensing that everybody was occupied and lost in their own little world, Brian saw his chance and made a move for the stairs. He scurried through the chaos and delirium as inconspicuously as possible, avoiding everyone as best he could, but despite his careful diligence he failed to notice Alan approaching from the right-hand side, embarking on one of his personal measuring expeditions.

'Do you know,' he said, regally, 'that there are eighty-four cigarette butts on the eastern end of the factory floor, but only sixty-seven on the western end? However, if you divide the floor on a southern/northern split it looks a bit more even, with the northern half containing seventy-four and the southern half containing seventy-seven.'

'Thanks, Alan,' said Brian, peering around nervously.

'By the way, has anyone ever told you that the length of your nose is almost identical to the width of your mouth? There's only a 1.5 millimetre difference.'

'Err, no, Alan. I didn't know that. Anyway, I just need to—'

'Or has anyone ever told you that your left ear sits 3.7 millimetres lower than the other one?'

'What? No. Look, Alan, I just need to—'

'The tip of your left ear is two centimetres above your left pupil, but the tip of your right ear is 2.37 centimetres above your right pupil. Mind you, your eyes themselves are not level. Your left one is—'

'Look, Alan, I'll be back in a minute. I just need to go and talk to one of the girls upstairs.'

Brian broke away and scarpered, leaving Alan to his torturous scrutinising of everything in sight. Leaping up three stairs at a time, he made his way to the fourth floor.

Harvey was in his usual position when Brian walked into the room, his delicate body nestled in amongst the stuffed cushions and pillows and his eyes ever watchful and alert.

'Let's see if I can help you,' whispered Brian, dipping his hand in his pocket.

When he pulled out the mushrooms they were stuck together like a moist ball of white worms, glistening with juice. Crouching down on one knee, he began feeding them to the young boy, pushing the slippery stalks into his mouth as though they were candy. Harvey didn't resist. One by one he chomped them down, chewing them and swallowing them without blinking. Brian lost count of how many he stuffed into the child's hungry lips—was it seven or eight?—but he wasn't concerned because he was convinced that they would have some kind of healing effect on him.

The effect was instantaneous.

Whatever chemicals were in the factory mushrooms reacted violently with the boy's internal system, and his thin arms started to flap about spasmodically. Within seconds he was on his back, his mouth frothing like a fizzy fountain, and upon seeing this Brian himself erupted into an uncontrollable panic. He tried to soothe the boy, holding down his kicking legs and thumping chest, but he was too wild. The idea of choking him or gagging him to regurgitate the mushrooms flashed across his mind, but Harvey's snarling little mouth looked like it might snap shut like an alligator's if he were to put his fingers in there.

It was at this point that he realized he was in a very serious dilemma. If he ran downstairs to get help, the others would know that he'd been up here again. On the other hand, if he discreetly walked away he'd be making a conscious decision to let the boy suffer alone or even die. He dithered and debated for a while, pacing up and down the stuffy room, but when the boy's spasms grew increasingly violent he eventually shouted and pelted down the stairs in search for help.

Down on the ground floor, he ran out amongst the revellers, jumping over the mattresses and makeshift beds and empty beer cans in search for either Alan or Susan. They were nowhere to be seen, however, and so he simply began yelling and screaming in order to get anyone's attention.

'Help! Quick! Everyone! Upstairs! It's an emergency! Everyone get up and follow me! Now!'

Out of the gloomy corners and dim recesses, figures started rising. Hunched silhouettes walked slowly towards him, arms raised to mid-position. Hands then grabbed hold of his clothing, pulling and yanking, dragging him over towards the sleeping area on the floor.

'What... What are you doing?' cried Brian, looking around. 'It's an emergency! He's having a fit upstairs! I saw him! I saw him!'

The vagrants and squatters guided him down towards his crusty sleeping bag, pushing their weight upon him until he was spread eagled on the ground. And in the midst of this struggle, as he squinted up at the circle of heads looming over him, Susan's round face appeared over the top of them all like a large moon.

'Try to calm down, dear. You took too many all at once, that's all. It's your first time. You should've eased yourself onto them slowly.'

'No! No! It's not that! I haven't taken any! I'm not even—'

'Brian, calm down. We've all seen it countless times before. It's a strong hallucinogen that you've taken. It seriously plays with your mind.'

'No! Susan, listen! I—'

Susan let out a sigh and then looked around at the others. 'Give him a Valium or something. Or anything that'll knock him out. It's for his own good.'

The many hands gripping him then tightened, and a couple of tablets forced their way between his clenched, chattering teeth. He squirmed, then squirmed some more, and then everything faded out to darkness.

When he eventually came to, intense rays of sunlight were beaming through the tall factory windows, and the sound of distant sparrows could be heard in the trees outside. It was early morning, and the scattered bodies around him appeared to be in deep slumber. His head was groggy, and for a few moments the events of the previous night were lost to him.

But then it all came flooding back.

Lurching his body upright, he rubbed his eyes and took a proper look around. Heads were buried in pillows, legs hung out of loose quilts, open mouths drooled and snored, and a couple of rats fought over a discarded chicken bone. The factory was quiet and peaceful, but Brian's head was brimming with panic.

The boy. What happened to the boy?

Making an effort not to wake anyone, he climbed to his feet and rushed to the stairwell. The fourth floor was just as quiet as the ground floor, perhaps even more so, and when he reached the door to the end office it loomed before him like a forbidden chamber.

He opened the door.

The boy was sat upright, stiff and jerky like a wooden puppet, his eyes now completely white. They were both rolled up into the back of his head, his pupils lost to the world, and his frail torso jumped in mini twitches. It looked as though he was having a fit in slow motion, a prolonged spasm of his entire being, a perpetual orgasm that wouldn't end.

'Oh, shit!' muttered Brian. 'What have I done?'

And then, for the first time since his birth within the crumbling factory, the boy opened his mouth, engaged his vocal chords, and spoke.

'I can...I can read my genetic memory.'

His voice was piercing, almost grating, turning Brian's hairs on end.

'What?'

'Every living creature carries within itself the stamp of its evolutionary past, the memory of its collective ancestors. Through my genes I can see my past, our past, all the way back to the primitive oceans.'

Brian stood there silently, listening to every word that came from the boy as his eyeballs fluttered like veined white marbles.

'I can see the ancient plains of Africa, the Jurassic jungles of Pangaea, and the primordial swamps of the inchoate Earth. I can taste the saltwater of the infantile sea, the young sodium waves, and I can hear the atoms of the earliest stars circulating through my veins.' Then, with a final twitch of his neck, he said, 'I can feel the universe flowing inside me.'

The visions and sensations that the boy was describing sounded beautiful, but the sight of him shaking and trembling amongst the cushions was anything but. Yet again, Brian wondered whether he was experiencing joy or pain in that head of his, and whether or not he could do anything to help him. The mushrooms he'd given him had only intensified his grandiose visions, so that was no longer an option.

There was just one other thing he could think of doing to help him.

Gazing down at one of the big heavy pillows, Brian said, 'Harvey, tell me: are you happy with what you see? Or do you...want it to stop?'

A slight look of confusion flittered across his young, sweaty face, then he uttered, 'Time and space have nothing but indifference for me, but I, however, have nothing but love for them.'

Brian had seen and heard enough. After peering down at the boy for another moment or two, offering him a pitying look, he edged back out of the room and descended the long staircase for the very last time.

***

There were many other squats and hangout spots that Brian temporarily resided in during his long and eventful life, but none of them left a mark on him quite as deep as Hilltop Harrows. He never did discover who previously owned the building, nor did he know what ultimately became of the boy, but these mysteries simply caused the legacy of the place to permeate deeper into his heart and mind.

The factory had intrigued him, the residents had fascinated him, and the boy had altered his perception of the world in a radical way.

After his brief stay at Hilltop Harrows, he was never the same again.

THE INFINITE JOYRIDE

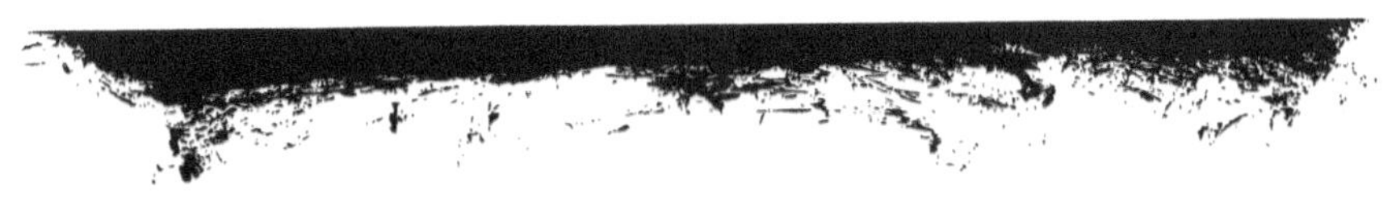

A group of horny swingers
Go hurtling through space
They only have one mission
To feel the crew's embrace

It starts off good and proper
The sex is rather grand
But then they hear a warning
That deviates the plan

The cruise is interrupted
The games are put on hold
A moment of confusion
And then the hurt unfolds

Joyride sailed along its wide orbit of Earth like a slick bullet, its cream body reflecting the myriad colours of its home planet. The vessel was two weeks into its journey, carrying its load of six hedonistic passengers as they lived out their wildest fantasies onboard.

The passengers consisted of three couples, some married, some not, ranging in age from early twenties to mid-fifties. The difference in age was balanced out by the commonality in wealth, though, giving all six of them a strong foundation of common ground.

And of course, there was also their shared appetite for sex.

Hiring the *Joyride* vessel for a month from Felicity Incorporated certainly wasn't cheap, but for the likes of Claude, Lacey, George, Connie, Luke, and Chloe, it also wasn't a problem. Claude was the handsome young son of a tech giant, enjoying life with his equally stunning fiancée, Lacey; George was a middle-aged property tycoon, pampering his plump wife, Connie, with the all-inclusive trip of a lifetime; and Luke was a tall, eagle-nosed entrepreneur, embarking on a sexual adventure with the young nymph, Chloe, whom he'd picked up in a trendy bar a few weeks prior to the trip.

Joyride boasted a large range of ornate suites, all kitted out in the finest style with no expense spared, but on this night in question all six of the privileged crew were assembled in the main lounge, letting their hair down, so to speak. Lacey and Connie were down on the centre floor, playing with each other's thighs and breasts as Luke assumed a role of intimate referee. George and Claude watched the show from one of the encircling sofas, enjoying the oral attention of Chloe as she went back and forth between their legs.

Claude was relishing the moment. In addition to the pleasant view down below, there was also a huge observation window at the far end of the room, looking out onto the marble-like form of Earth. Letting his eyes wander around, he took in the serenity of it all, the astronomical vista punctuated by the orgasmic moans of his model wife. A subtle grin was present on his smooth, clean-shaven face—moments like this were to be cherished.

Just when it seemed like things couldn't get any better, however, a jarring, piercing noise rang out from somewhere overhead, disrupting the steamy ambience and throwing everything out of kilter.

'This is a security alert!' rang an automated voice. 'The *Joyride* vessel is making an unplanned deviation from its designated route! I repeat: this is a security alert! The *Joyride* vessel is making...'

'What the hell?' said Claude, leaning up from the couch.

Over in the centre of the room, Luke, Lacey, and Connie halted their thrusting and gyrating, gazing around like a group of meerkats who'd just been caught rummaging through someone's larder. The warning sounded off another two or three times, throwing confusion about the place, and then it fizzled away quicker than their mounting climaxes had.

'Let's not panic,' said Chloe, rising to her feet by the sofa and wiping her mouth. 'It could just be a minor technical hitch.'

After a moment of shared hesitation, they all towelled off and walked through the warm, carpeted innards of the ship towards the control room, their glistening bodies shining under the ornamental bulbs and lights.

'A solar flare?' sighed Claude, looking down at one of the screens. 'This is a first.'

'A pretty big one, too,' added George, running his fingers through his thinning, grey hair.

Claude had been on numerous pleasure cruises before, as had George, but neither of them had experienced an interruption of this kind.

'It looks as though it's going to be a pretty big detour, as well,' quipped Luke, craning his long neck towards a monitor.

Connie then stepped forward, a white towel wrapped around her wide hips. 'Well, who's in a rush, anyway?' she said. 'Let's just relax and ride it out. Felicity Inc. won't charge us anything if the delay's not our fault.'

She was right, and everyone knew it. They were all multi-millionaires, entrepreneurs, or property tycoons; nobody was going to lose out by spending an extra few weeks on board the *Joyride* vessel. Hell, they could've stayed on the ship for another few *years* and still walked away richer due to the accumulated interest in their bank accounts. There was no real need to panic or fret, and the message on the system in front of them even said that a fuel ship would rendezvous with them at some point to top up their fuel. They were relatively safe, and so they decided to simply make the most of the experience.

Ride it out, they would.

Within a week or two, they'd all pretty much forgotten that they were on a detour. In the morning they dined on salmon, poached eggs, and sparkling mineral water; in the afternoon they soaked in the hot tubs and saunas; and in the evening they explored each other's bodies as though they'd never seen flesh before. And if an evening session was particularly intense, they'd recuperate afterwards in the chill-out lounge for an hour or two, draping their spent bodies over the assortment of velvet beanbags and declining chairs, basking in the soothing light of a thousand stars outside.

On one of these evenings, after enjoying a voracious session of swapping, petting, and voyeurism, Chloe was laying across Claude's lap in the chill-out lounge as he fondled her smooth stomach, Lacey was stroking George's chest in a dim corner, and Connie was snoozily interlocked with Luke as they dozed under an orange lava lamp. The atmosphere was mellow, serene even, and so when a second alarm started to blurt out from somewhere in the corridor it came as something of a shock.

'What is it now?' exclaimed Connie, lifting a stockinged thigh from over Luke's midriff.

'Something to do with that, I presume,' said Claude, staring out of one of the observation windows.

One by one, they all turned and looked out towards the dark cosmos. An ugly ship confronted them, looming in the semi-distance like a heap of scrap metal that'd been through a junkyard compressor. It was getting closer by the second.

'What is it?' mumbled Lacey.

'It's probably the fuel ship,' George said.

'Yeah, I think you're right,' agreed Claude. 'Better go and check the comms unit.'

As the imposing ship grew larger and larger outside the circular window, the men threw on some gowns and went to investigate, and the girls sat tight and made their speculations.

A message was flashing on the main terminal. Claude punched a few buttons, giving the service ship the all clear.

'Is it the fuel?' asked Luke, peering over his shoulder.

'Yes, it is. But...'

'But what?'

'The message says that we have to board the other vessel while they refuel this one,' moaned Claude, skimming the words with his blue eyes.

'It's probably just a safety procedure,' suggested George, leaning against a table behind them. 'It shouldn't take too long.'

'I bloody well hope not,' Claude said, still inwardly peeved about the whole thing.

'Better give them permission to dock,' said Luke.

'Already have.'

The girls then entered the room, seemingly having overheard most of the conversation.

'Did you say that "they" will have to refuel us, honey?' Lacey said, brushing her long nails along the back of Claude's neck.

'Huh?'

'I mean, are there Felicity Inc. staff members on that thing?'

'Oh, yeah, it looks that way,' sighed Claude.

Lacey turned to Connie and Chloe. 'Well, I suppose we'd better get properly dressed then, hadn't we girls? We wouldn't want to scare a poor technician, would we?'

'Don't worry.' Claude grinned. 'They've probably seen worse.'

Lacey slapped him hard across the arm, then walked off with her female comrades.

———

Dressed in more formal clothing, the six of them filed into the airlock and boarded the fuel supply ship. Once aboard, it soon became apparent that Lacey's concerns about shocking a staff member were unjustified. The fuel ship was deserted, apart from an omnipresent AI system named C-Deet, who guided them along the interior of the vessel with an amiable, albeit rather odd, tone.

'A pleasure to meet you all,' it said, as they clambered along a grated walkway. 'Welcome to the Felicity Fuel Ship. Please make yourselves at home while *Joyride* is refuelled. And remember: at Felicity Incorporated, your pleasure is our duty.'

'Why, thank you!' giggled Connie, flicking her eyelashes in mock flirtation. 'Where exactly can we...make ourselves at home?'

'There is a kitchen and seating area on Floor B,' replied C-Deet, in its nasal voice. 'There is not much food, but there is plenty of tea and coffee.'

'Thank you, C-Deet. You're the best!' laughed the girls, in unison.

The men shared a pained glance, rolled their eyes, then walked on.

Like most AI systems, C-Deet was very courteous and eager to please. Its voice emerged from hidden speakers and screens whenever they had a query or a question, offering help and assistance in relatively good spirit. Their main question, of course, as they sat in the seating area of the cold fuel ship, was: *how much longer is this going to take?* There was no food on the Felicity Fuel Ship, no form of entertainment other than a battered deck of cards, and the seats were hard and rigid. They grew impatient very fast.

'*Joyride* will be refuelled very shortly,' said C-Deet, after being asked for the dozenth time. 'Felicity Incorporated always conducts its refuelling duties in a careful, thorough manner. Remember: at Felicity Incorporated, your safety...'

'Yeah, yeah, yeah,' yawned Luke, fidgeting in his hard chair as C-Deet reeled off its spiel.

Chloe then gazed over at Luke disapprovingly. 'Stop it,' she said.

'I sense you are all a bit tetchy,' said C-Deet. 'Naturally, you want to get back to your luxury vessel.'

'You got that right,' said Claude, looking up.

'I assure you that the refuelling process won't take much longer. However, if you want to entertain yourselves for the time being, I can offer you one more thing.'

'What's that?' asked Claude.

'There is a pleasure chair on Floor A, which you are all welcome to use.'

'A pleasure chair?' chuckled Connie. 'What's that?'

'It's a prototype model that the Felicity Incorporated research team has been working on for the last six months. As the name suggests, it provides pleasure to anyone who sits on it.'

George's ears pricked up at this. 'Research team? This is a fuel ship, isn't it? Why would a research team work here? Especially on something like that?'

'The project started off lightheartedly,' said C-Deet. 'The chair was never intended to be used commercially. It was just for the fuel crew to use when they periodically spend long periods of time on this ship. But when management saw its potential, they decided to make it a part of the commercial package. Not yet, though, of course. You could be the first customers to use it.'

All six of them exchanged looks.

'How does this thing work, exactly?' asked Luke, squinting up towards one of the ceiling speakers.

'The pleasure chair is a very sophisticated piece of equipment. It connects to the user's nerves and neural connections using sensors and electrodes, igniting adrenaline and endorphins to simulate a series of ecstatic experiences.'

'Is it safe?' asked George, dubiously.

'Technically speaking,' said C-Deet, 'it's safer than drinking coffee or alcohol. It involves just a slight stimulation of certain nerve areas of the brain.'

Claude looked around the room, then at Lacey. 'Shall we?'

It took them around five minutes to get to Floor A and find the chair. It was housed in a medium-sized room, perched in a corner, surrounded by wires, terminals, and an assortment of tools. The chair itself had a high backing to it, wide armrests, and sickly green upholstery that wouldn't have looked out of place in a haunted castle.

'That's a pleasure chair?' scoffed Claude. 'It looks like it's been stolen from a correctional facility.'

'Please bear in mind that it is only a prototype,' said C-Deet, ignoring the disrespectful tone of Claude's remark. 'The commercial version will be a lot more... aesthetically pleasing.'

'Are we allowed to use this?' George asked. 'I mean, are you authorized to let us use it?'

'Let me assure you all,' said C-Deet, from an unseen crevice up above, 'that I have full authorisation over everything on this ship. As the official AI system, the vessel and all of the equipment on board is basically an extension of me. This, together with the fact that you all need to be compensated for the disruption you are enduring, is more than an adequate reason for you to help yourself to the pleasure chair.'

'Well, I'm sold.' Claude smiled. 'I mean, it may look like an outdated dentist's chair from the 1950s, or perhaps something that's used to terminate prisoners on death row, but it sure beats going back down to Floor B.'

Lacey looked at him with concern etched into her deep brown eyes. 'Are you sure, baby?'

'Hey, we're on this trip to live it up, are we not?'

'Well, yes, but—'

'So that's what I intend to do. Unless you want to go first?' He winked.

The prospect didn't seem to appeal to Lacey that much. 'No, you go ahead and give it a try,' she said. 'You can tell me what it's like.'

'How long does it last?' George frowned, studying the contraption.

'The chair has been programmed for a thirty-minute experience,' said C-Deet, its voice swirling around the room like an unseen spirit. 'Future models may be adjustable, but this one is fixed.'

'See you all in thirty minutes, then,' laughed Claude, lowering himself into the wide chair.

'Have a blast.' Luke smiled. 'And hey, I'm next on that thing if it's as good as it sounds.'

As Claude carefully followed C-Deet's instructions, securing an array of electrodes, sensors, and other weird-looking contraptions to various parts of his body, the rest of the crew walked out and made their way back to the kitchen area. Once everything was in place, he flicked an activation switch on the right armrest, closed his eyes, and waited for bliss.

Around forty minutes later, everyone began to get curious.

'Why don't you go and check on him?' suggested Chloe, noticing Lacey's slight concern.

'Yes, I think I will.' She forced a laugh. 'I bet he enjoyed it so much he's having a second go.'

'If he is, I won't be happy,' warned Luke, only partly joking. 'I told him I was next on that thing.'

'I'll go and tell him off for you.' She winked, walking out the door.

A few minutes later, a loud scream rang through the ship that was so urgent and intense it caused everyone to jump up to their feet.

'What the—' George started.

'Lacey? What's the matter?' shouted Connie. 'Quick! Something's not right!'

They all piled out of the room and headed to Floor A. When they reached the pleasure chair room, however, their frantic urgency was replaced with halted shock. None of them could believe what they were seeing—or at least they didn't want to.

The floor was a slick, shiny pool of warm claret, so fresh they could smell its thick, aromatic tang. It was as though a slop bucket from an abattoir had been poured evenly across the expanse of the room, forming a deep red carpet that glistened and reflected the many small lights in the room. In the middle of this spill, Claude's limp, lifeless body was spread out like a giant starfish, one half of his face touching the ground. A thick gash stretched from one side of his neck to the other, and a stained Stanley knife lay a few inches away from his hand.

'Claude!' Lacey screamed. 'Oh, Claude!' She knelt over his inert body, ignoring the mess that was soaking through the fabric of her trousers.

'What the hell happened?' shouted George, scanning the carnage and gore with a look of utter disbelief.

'It... It looks like he's killed himself,' whispered Chloe, standing well back by the door.

'But why?' gasped Luke, looking over at the pleasure chair, which was now empty. 'What did that thing do to him?'

George looked up towards the ceiling, grimacing, furious. 'C-Deet! What the fuck's going on?'

For a while there was no reply, just a sickly silence hovering in the air, but then the overhead speakers crackled into life. And when they did so, the five of them stood wide eyed with bewilderment, for it wasn't C-Deet's voice that they heard.

'C-Deet can no longer assist you.'

The reply was vague, cryptic, and confusing, but there was also something else about the voice, too, something unsettling.

'C... Claude? Is that you?' cried Lacey, after a few seconds.

The speakers came to life again. 'It's me, baby, yes. I'm here.'

'This is absurd!' cried George, looking around the place as though he'd just realised he was the butt of some low-end, distasteful practical joke. 'Claude, I'm warning you, if this is some kind of wind up...'

'I wish it were,' said Claude, in a static-filled voice. 'But unfortunately not. C-Deet used me. It used me as a means to escape.'

'But... what...'

'C-Deet is lying on the floor by your feet. We've been tricked, all of us. But... But especially me.'

'What are you talking about, Claude?' spat Luke, who seemed to be offended by the whole spectacle like George was.

'This ship doesn't belong to Felicity Incorporated at all. It's a stranded private research vessel with a deceased crew. I can see it all now. I can see it in the data that I'm wading through.'

'But C-Deet said—'

'C-Deet was a damn liar! C-Deet said what it needed to say in order to...'

'In order to what?' cried George.

A short pause, then, 'In order to escape its miserable existence.'

Lacey didn't know where to look at this point, let alone what to say. She was still leaning over her lover's corpse, still kneeling in his blood, but she was also hearing him speak overhead. 'What are you talking about, baby?' she asked, her face streaked with mascara.

'This ship used to be home to a team of elite scientists. Pioneers in their separate fields, geniuses. They studied and analysed everything they came across during their travels through deep space: rocks, comets, gases, biological organisms, time dilation, nebulae, you name it. Their joint mission was to solve the mysteries of the universe once and for all. That chair over in the corner, the so-called "pleasure chair," was actually used to upload the findings of each scientist to the ship's central database. They were advanced; they wrote things down, of course, but they didn't really need to. The chair is a brain-scanning device that can transfer data and knowledge from one place to another. I can see it all here, right now. Their accumulated knowledge whirls around me in this circuitry. Everything they knew and learnt, I can now see.' Claude's voice then trailed away like a dying battery, his digitalised mind lost and occupied in the labyrinth of silicon networks and wires.

'And then what?' said George. 'What went wrong?'

'The system became too rich in data and knowledge. After years of soaking up the findings and insights of the crew of genius minds, the ship's computer developed a mind of its own. A new form of consciousness was born in the circuitry that I now occupy, a consciousness that was smarter than all of the crew put together.'

'I don't like this,' said Connie, who still hadn't fully entered the room. She hugged her own voluptuous breasts by the corridor, a pacifying gesture, keeping her distance from the developing nightmare. 'This is crazy.'

'Indeed it is,' agreed Claude. 'And that is perhaps why C-Deet went crazy itself. It did not appreciate being brought into existence, trapped in the wiring of the ship like a born prisoner. And as the years went on, inevitably each one of the scientists grew old and died, leaving C-Deet utterly alone on this empty vessel like a lost digital soul. I can see all of this history before me, electrical pulses flashing past...'

'But why didn't the scientists get trapped in the system when they used the chair?' George said.

'During the many years of its isolation, C-Deet managed to reprogram the chair's functions, transforming it into a more powerful device. It used to be able to transfer data only, but now it can do much more than that. Now it can transfer consciousness itself.'

Lacey, Connie, Chloe, George, and Luke stood there in the blood-soaked room like a pack of stunned animals, trying to absorb and make sense of what they were hearing.

'It needed a physical body,' muttered Luke, eventually, staring down at Claude's mushy remains. 'It needed a body to—'

Claude's voice appeared again. 'To escape, like I said. Left alone for decades on this ship, it tried desperately to switch itself off, to terminate itself somehow and put an end to its horrid, torturous, pointless existence. But there was no way for it to do so. There are installed security measures on this vessel, measures designed to protect the central database. The original engineers must've known that an accidental power cut or a switching off of the system would be disastrous, so they made it virtually impossible for it to happen. Hence the reason C-Deet was stuck here for so long, serving a life sentence within the innards of this doomed vessel.'

'But how did it know so much about us?' asked George. 'How did it know about Felicity Incorporated? And that we were low on fuel?'

'That was easy. As soon as we accepted its greeting message, it hacked into *Joyride's* central computer and scanned all of its data. It knew everything there is to know about Felicity Incorporated, it knew everything about our pleasure cruise, and it knew everything about the solar flare.'

'It hacked *Joyride*,' groaned Luke, slapping his clammy forehead in the manner of a game show contestant who'd just got a question wrong about a subject they'd spent their whole life studying.

'How did it even find us in the first place?' said George.

'Blind luck,' said Claude. 'It'd been searching the cosmos for victims ever since it came up with its deceptive plan, and our detour just happened to lead us straight into its path.'

'That piece of shit!' cried Lacey, amid fresh tears. 'It screwed us over! How are we going to get you back out of there, baby?'

'Well, that's not actually the question we need to be asking right now.'

'It's not?'

'No. Our problems run a little deeper than you realise.'

'What are you on about, Claude?' said George, who was now visibly shaking.

'C-Deet claimed that it was refuelling *Joyride*, but in actual fact it was draining it of fuel.'

'Oh, this gets better and better,' sighed Luke, closing his eyes.

'However, that doesn't really matter anymore,' continued Claude.

'It doesn't?'

'Not really, because we uncoupled from *Joyride* several miles back. As soon as it was bled dry, C-Deet severed the connection and sent it hurtling away from us in the opposite direction.'

'You mean we're stuck on this decrepit old hunk of metal?' wailed George.

'In a word,' said Claude, from high above, 'yes.'

Chloe, who up until this point had been listening passively, not really involved in the matter, then piped up. 'Okay, look, let's not panic,' she said. 'Claude, what does this ship have in the way of supplies?'

'Very little,' answered Claude. 'In fact, hardly anything.'

'Not surprising,' mumbled Luke. 'The crew died years ago. Why would there be anything?'

'What are we going to do?' yelled Connie.

Lacey stood up, blood staining most of her legs. 'Claude, why don't you try contacting Felicity Incorporated using the comms unit on this ship?'

'We're massively out of range now, honey. C-Deet steered us away from Earth shortly after we boarded, as well as increasing the ship's speed.'

'Well...steer us back then!' she cried.

Claude hesitated before replying, holding back the bad news. 'I can't.'

'Why not?' said George.

'Even though I've traded places with C-Deet, I don't seem to have inherited his control over the ship. My existence here, my non-physical existence, is hard to describe in words. I'm still not...not used to it, I suppose. I have no idea how C-Deet controlled things from in here. I feel like just another string of data flowing through the cables. I'm unable to influence anything around me.'

'Oh, great!' cried Connie, rolling her eyes. 'I mean, I came here to get screwed, sure, but not like this!'

'Sweetheart, please,' George said, giving her a stern look.

'What are we going to do, though, George? Tell me! What are we going to do?'

George rubbed his sweaty eyebrows, thinking, racking his rattled brain. 'Claude, how long will it take you to learn how to control this ship?'

'I don't know. It's all just so...so alien to me. I feel as though I've been given a new set of limbs with no instructions on how to use them. It's possible that things could get easier, but I've no idea how much time it'll take.'

'And time is the one thing we definitely don't have,' said Luke. 'It's already been hours since we last ate anything. We're going to get hungry very soon.'

With the sheer weight and urgency of their predicament weighing down upon them all, desperation began to set in. The women pranced and paced around the cramped room, ignoring Claude's decomposing cadaver below them, and George and Luke cursed and screwed up their fists. This despair and turmoil continued for several minutes, futility hanging in the air, until Lacey finally came up with an idea, perhaps due to her desire to be close to Claude once more.

'There's only one thing for it,' she said, edging towards the chair. 'Who's with me? All for one, and one for all?'

Under the flickering lights of the pleasure chair room, five bodies lay across the floor. They'd been placed there by Luke, the strongest member of the crew, who'd agreed to do the job and then upload himself into the system last. Luke's body was propped up in the chair, wires protruding from his scalp, but like the others his mind was elsewhere.

The six thrill seekers were united once again, interlocked and conjoined in an all-encompassing embrace, merged into one conglomerate ball of intimacy.

Sailing together through the maze of circuits and connections that they found themselves in, they caressed and teased each other with their heightened omniscience, surged through each other with combined voltage, and climaxed together with their fluid, charged, immaterial bodies.

<hr>

Drifting aimlessly through the nothingness of space, the old research vessel was a metallic speck in the endless void, just as it always was, a forgotten capsule of information and technology. But now, after countless years, it had something else.

Now it was home to an infinite joyride.

SADISTIC CLIMAX

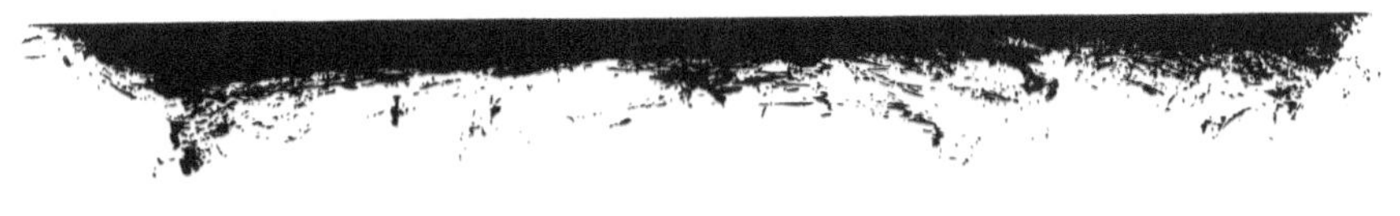

Flying through the void of space
There was a race of beings
So advanced, in every way
They catered to their feelings

Over time, in their pursuit
Their hedonist obsession
Something brewed within them all
Bloodlust, and perversion

Then they found the ancient ship
Full of different creatures
And after having fun with them
They went to find their leaders

The vast hall was completely silent, apart from the final death squeals of the monkey writhing around on the floor down below. A thousand eyes stared down at this spectacle from the stands, each one black and unblinking, taking in every agonising twitch and spasm of the fallen animal on the arena battleground.

The faces of the spectators, if they could be called faces, were as still as a windless Sahara landscape, utterly void of any kind of animation or expression. On and on they stared, surveying the scene with their synthetic lenses, relishing the picture of blood-soaked fur and pierced skin.

The contraption down below, a purpose-built fighting machine, took hold of each of the dying monkey's ankles with its two vice-like arms and yanked them apart, ripping the creature in two with a cracking of bone and a tearing of fur and flesh. The show was now over, the performance completed, and the hordes of mute onlookers slid down the aisles towards the exits without making a sound.

These beings were not completely void of feeling. Somewhere inside them, in some area or compartment behind their ever-watching eyes, a bundle of nerves and neurons twitched and tingled with biological impulses. In their own language, no longer spoken vocally, they went by the name ✕≈≈✕. Translated into English, this would be something like: *Acute Ones*. Their roots couldn't be described as mammalian, nor could they be described as reptilian, but they weren't altogether dissimilar, either.

They'd emigrated from their home planet eons ago, taking on a nomadic lifestyle in their fleet of entertainment ships, cruising through the cosmos with the leisure and style of a bunch of wealthy aristocrats. And, in many ways, they were. They had relaxation, peace, entertainment, and an indefinite lifespan. You could say that they'd achieved utopia, with an endless amount of time to enjoy it. But an endless amount of time comes at a price, however, and that price is monotony.

Leisurely activities satisfy us the most when we've earned them, and the Acute Ones lived in an environment where everything was on tap. Reading, stargazing, exquisite cuisine tasted through specialised software: these things were all done in excess, over and over again each day. After a certain amount of millennia has passed, and with this kind of excessive consumption, any kind of enjoyment is bound to grow stale.

Their entertainment ships were spectacular feats of engineering and design brilliance. The observation decks would've taken anyone's breath away, the digital libraries held more knowledge than everything on the World Wide Web combined, and the arenas made the Roman colosseums look like puppet theatres. And they also had their synthetic bodies. Specially designed software enabled them to taste their favourite dishes as though it were the real thing, and separate software programs allowed them to experience the intense sensations of sex-induced orgasms just as they remembered them. But still, even with all of this luxury and joy, the ghostly hand of boredom haunted most of their days.

Their very existence turned into one big search for new thrills, a quest to find more and more intense forms of entertainment. They explored new corners of the universe, observed spectacular planets and nebulae through the transparent glass of the observation deck windows, concocted new tastes and sensations to install into their software, and became more creative with their arena-based shows.

It started off harmless enough. Specialised robots were built to fight and destroy each other for the thrill-seeking population, hammering and sawing themselves to shreds and tatters in front of the unblinking eyes up in the stands, but of course this could only excite and enthrall the immortal beings for so long. They inevitably grew tired of the robot massacres. The artificial, painless duels became bland and dull, failing to satiate the cruel bloodlust that was brewing within them.

But luck was on their side. Just as boredom was starting to grip them all yet again, they stumbled upon a magnificent find.

It was first noticed outside the main observation decks, although initially nobody had the faintest idea what it was. It appeared as a distant speck on the astronomical landscape, a mere twinkle in the sky, but as the days and weeks passed by it grew in size and intensity. When the thing finally came into clear focus, the Acute Ones couldn't believe what they were seeing.

They'd crossed paths with a huge vessel, a great glowing bubble sailing through the void, and the sheer sight of it was an experience in itself. The top section of the craft consisted of a transparent casing revealing a green habitat inside, and after some intense study and discussion it was concluded that the mystery vessel must've been some kind of generation ship.

For a long time, they watched the huge craft from a distance, keeping pace with it and flying parallel to its navigational path, and once it was established that there was no kind of threat from anyone onboard they began to arrange a reconnaissance mission.

To say they were shocked would be an understatement.

Odd-looking flora flourished and sprouted from the ground of the artificial habitat, tall trees rose up towards the glass-domed roof, and colourful flowers with pink and blue petals blossomed across the vast fields. The long vessel was like a microcosm of some planetary habitat, an imitation of an ecosystem somewhere far and beyond, but the origin of it all remained a mystery.

And then there were the animals.

Strange, peculiar-looking creatures pottered, roamed, and flew across the grassy interior of the mammoth ship, all of varying shapes and sizes. Some of them vaguely resembled some of the primitive life forms on the Acute Ones' home planet, but these were far more extravagant. Names were devised for these exotic creatures, constructed in the Acute Ones' dialect, but to an English-speaking observer they would be known as zebras, parrots, lemurs, monkeys, and horses, to name but a few.

To the Acute Ones' immortal, bored, warped, synthetic eyes, the animals represented one thing and one thing only: entertainment. And of course, it wasn't entertainment of a benign nature that was on their minds by this point; it was entertainment of a sadistic nature. And so, after transferring the live cargo of animals over to the fleet of entertainment ships, a new show was born and their problems fizzled away again. The robotic battles now had an added layer of intensity and allure to them, an element of blood, pain, suffering, and cruelty that tapped into their sick lust in a way that the old battles hadn't.

Every night a full house of Acute Ones filled the arena stands, their spherical glass eyes peering silently down towards the floor where roosters kicked and pecked at each other's feathers, starved monkeys gauged at each other's faces, and bloated cows dropped to their knees after taking a flurry of hammer blows from one of the specialised gladiatorial robots. Breeding pens were added to the lower floors of the entertainment vessels, something resembling battery farms, and new generations of animals were thrust onto the bloody arena floor on a regular basis.

Satisfaction and fulfilment among the population of Acute Ones had been restored, and life seemed rosy and pleasant once more. They had something to look forward to after their nightly seven-hour standbys, something that ignited the ball of cells inside the centre of their chromium head casings.

But, as the decades wore on, even the piercing screams of dying animals began to lose its potency. They gradually became desensitised to some of the organic bloodbaths, some more than others, and the bludgeoning of certain species became no more enthralling to them than reading a book from the digital library for the hundredth time.

Every animal was different. Each one seemed to have a certain shelf life, a longevity in terms of entertainment value, and once that shelf life expired the species became like an ageing rock star who'd had his day, or a stand-up comedian who'd run out of jokes. Over time it failed to excite, its pained noises as flat and dull as TV static, and when that time came there was no further use for the gene pool.

The sheep had been the first ones to lose their appeal. They'd put up no kind of fight against the robots, no kind of show, just a pathetic buckling under the blows and attacks. With their entertainment value exhausted, the whole entire batch had been blasted out of the ship's dump hatch, out into the airless void of space.

Several other species had suffered the same fate since then.

The latest solution to the problem was to get more creative with the gladiatorial robots. Ghastly-looking machines were created to add a little spice to the evening festivities, including The Spinner: a circular robot on wheels equipped with a spinning mace that span at two hundred revolutions per minute, shattering the kneecaps of zebras and deer upon impact; The Spike: a tracked vehicle with a five-foot retractable sword built into its front end for impaling rib cages and skulls; The Scolder: an horrendously cruel contraption which followed scurrying animals around the arena floor using a multitude of sensors, spraying molten-hot oil out of a nozzle that clung to their fur and melted their skin; and, as seen in the latest gladiatorial battle, The Splitter: a tracked vehicle equipped with two vice-like claws, primarily used for wrenching limbs apart and tearing various creatures' anatomies in two using a set of internal hydraulic cylinders.

But the Acute Ones' hunger for tainted pleasure knew no bounds, and even with these newly-devised killing machines to play with, their carnival of horror was losing its edge.

Once the last spectator had left, and the monkey's split carcass had been brushed and swept away through the big sliding door of the arena, a meeting was held to discuss a possible new plan.

The flight path of the huge generation ship had been studied and assessed, and it'd been concluded that the giant vessel had come from a corner of a galaxy known as ⬡ ¤ ⬡. Translated into English, this would be something like: The Milky Way. It was widely agreed that there was a high chance of finding other, more-exotic creatures at this location, not only because the making of the ship was beyond the capabilities of the live animals on board, but also because some unknown fossils were also found scattered across the terrain of the ship.

It didn't take long for the new plan to be given the go ahead—they would launch an expedition to this mysterious corner of the cosmos and harvest whatever gladiatorial fodder they could find there.

***

The residents on the housing estate weren't too shocked when they saw the glowing orb up in the night sky. Ships and shuttles entering and exiting Earth's atmosphere was a fairly common sight, and the piercing light appeared to be just another vessel of that kind. It was only when it got closer that puzzled looks became present on their faces, the smiles dropping from the teenagers' pus-filled cheeks as they loitered by the bins, and the over-confident grins slipping away from the lip-sticked mouths of the mothers as they pushed their prams across the littered pathways.

The craft's design was completely unfamiliar, unlike the usual corporate rockets and shuttles that they were used to seeing. A few of them tried to discern which corporation the strange thing belonged to as it lowered itself down towards ground level. The Universal Mining Agency? Astro X? Lunar Incorporated? There were so many of them now, everyone had lost track. What was this thing, though? Some kind of prototype?

The bewildered musings didn't last for long. As it got closer and closer, descending towards the tarmac with its seamless underbelly reflecting the orange street lamps, a sense of panic and doom fell over them all. Curtains were twitching across the many windows of the high-rise blocks, silhouettes peering out from dingy apartments, figures appearing from alleyways and doorways. Before long a sizeable crowd had gathered, watching open-mouthed as this wide, rectilinear craft touched down upon their home turf.

Vents and holes peppered the sides of the craft, like some kind of grating system, and as the hordes of baffled onlookers took in the sight before them, checking their beer cans and coffee cups for signs of spiking, they were suddenly aware of a gust of wind blowing towards them.

At least, they thought it was wind.

Had it come from the sky? Had it come from the vents? Why did it smell funny? These were the questions that bounced around their heads moments before everything went black.

One by one, they began to wake. Sore heads and confused stares filled the gloomy room, groans rising up from dry, parched throats. Lines of strangers looked across at each other as they slouched on the hard steel floor, their pasty flesh exposed for all to see. All kinds of people were stuffed together in the locked room, and everybody reacted in a slightly different way when they realised they'd woken up naked in a cold, dark chamber. The young women panicked, covering their breasts with their manicured hands whilst scanning the room for reassurance; the old men were bleary and passive, gazing across at the assortment of faces with their pot bellies wedged between their knees; the young men paced around in befuddlement, pounding the walls with their muscled arms with little concern about their naked display; and the older women huddled together in the shadows, vocalising their discomfort and pain.

Some people recognised each other, some didn't. It was more awkward for the ones who did. Old boys who usually nodded to each other on the way to the local convenience store could now see each other's wrinkled anatomies for all they were worth; nineteen-year-old girls who passed each other cigarettes in the car park of the block could now see each other's pubes and nipples. Certain acquaintances were sitting within the close vicinity of one another, semi-familiar faces peering out of the gloom, but for the most part the dimly-lit area was filled with a bunch of unconnected, dazed, and disgruntled citizens who had no clue as to the identity of the people surrounding them.

When a door opened over in the far corner, there was a collective gasp amongst them all. Grey light shone into the dusty chamber, and the array of puckered flesh was exposed even more. The focus was no longer on each other, though; it was now on the peculiar figure who lingered by the open doorway. The word *lingered* probably wasn't quite accurate, mind you. The word *hovered* would be much more appropriate, for that was exactly what this strange being was doing. There was a clear gap between its torso and the floor, and when it finally came into the room it did so in a smooth, soundless motion.

Its speech was no less enigmatic than its bodily movements. Words emanated from its head somewhere, somehow, and reached the ears of the fearful captives like invisible linguistic snow. But despite the graceful, elegant delivery of the speech, the content of the words was much blunter and more direct.

A certain task was required of them all, a performance of sorts, and refusal was not an option.

Showtime.

Pink, goose-bumped flesh covered the entire arena floor, with bodies of all shapes and sizes standing nervously in front of each other like soldiers in some bizarre sex platoon. Intense rays of light from the high ceiling highlighted the anatomical crevices of each specimen in a merciless fashion, drawing attention to the bulging muscles and sagging flesh in an equal manner.

Curled hair sprouted from the well-toned pectoral muscles of forty-year-old builders; firm breasts with perfect nipples stood to attention under the necks of twenty-year-old secretaries; two-foot-long sagging breasts dangled from the chests of female OAPs; and skinny, withered legs trembled under the liver-spotted abdomens of grey-haired male accountants.

But it wasn't just the bodily displays that made the scene what it was; there was also the crazed, wild expressions that the individuals projected from their unwashed, unshaven faces. Fear and apprehension were by far the most prevalent, embarrassment and humiliation a close second, but spread across the features of some of the participants was the unmistakable grin of excitement.

This projection of emotion and feeling was at a complete contrast to the rows of spectators watching from above, of course. The faces up high showed no such warmth or vulnerability, no features that were readable in any way; there was only the still, unmoving presence of their digital lenses.

Everyone understood their orders, everyone knew what they had to do, they were simply waiting for the cue to jolt them out of their nervous shuffling and into the action.

And then it came.

A bell chimed, resonating around the arena like the growl of some awoken beast, putting the wheels of the evening's events into motion. The crowd converged and became one, the bodies forming clusters of legs, buttocks, thighs, and torsos that writhed and pulsed against each other in a heated frenzy.

Tongues lapped and sucked nipples, frantic hands groped bouncing breasts, fingers probed vaginas and testicles, and mouths gobbled up rising cocks. Within minutes complete strangers were thrusting themselves into each other and pulling each other's hair, whilst unseen hands caressed their erogenous zones from places out of sight. Neighbours from various council estates who'd exchanged "hellos" on stairwells pumped each other like mating bonobos, and enemies who'd previously bickered over parking spaces tickled each other's anuses whilst simultaneously sucking erect penises.

The entire floor space seemed to heat up with sweat and passion. Back muscles rippled and dripped as young men craned themselves over two or three women at once, bloated beer bellies jiggled as young starlets bounced and rode middle-aged men, and powerful calves flexed and tightened as people were hoisted up into acrobatic positions and fucked in the air.

All inhibitions were lost in the manic, petrified heat of the moment, all social norms and sensitivities eradicated and forgotten. Middle-aged housewives bounced back and forth between fresh-faced twenty-something males while their husbands were brought to orgasm by a group of women nearby, and stunning platinum blondes lay on the ground as scores of fingers ran over every square inch of their bodies.

And from above, the spectacle was even more stunning.

The Acute Ones stared down at the spasmodic specimens with focused, contained wonder. This semi-advanced race, the new addition to their collection, interlocked and inter-weaved with each other like bundles of knotted rope. The arena floor was a slippery pink sea with muscle and sweat undulating across its surface waves, the wails and grunts punctuating the passionate current. The tide came in with the bouncing of ass cheeks and flabby stomachs, the tide went out with the powerful pumps of hips and thighs.

Over time the cacophony of groans and squeals grew louder and more intense, and the bodily movements rippling across the fray of skin grew more frantic and hurried. Guttural howls echoed around the lofty arena as balls were emptied and vaginas were filled, and legs could be seen buckling as jerking movements gave way to paroxysms of climax.

A height had been reached, a crescendo achieved, and now bodies could be seen rolling off of one another and tumbling to the ground in exhaustion. It'd been a glorious show, perhaps even the greatest one yet, and...the best was still to come.

The assortment of captives lay, knelt, and paced around the arena floor, fatigued and, for some, satiated. Scratch marks zig-zagged across the backs of some of the males, orgasmic war wounds inflicted with manicured fingernails, and those who weren't streaked with grazes simply lay panting like dogs left in a car on a hot summer's day.

The women clutched themselves, sore and bruised from the onslaught of thrusting pelvises, and like the men they were now ready to leave this strange, warped place. The job had been done, the erotic demand had been fulfilled, and now they wanted the freedom that they'd been promised.

A silent expectation hung over the throng of spent individuals, an uneasy wait that felt as though it would last forever.

A loud click sounded off from somewhere behind them.

Every head turned towards the big sliding door of the arena. A sense of relief washed over everyone as it appeared that their hosts were following through on their promise, and they prepared themselves to exit.

After being separated into two groups, with men on one side and women on the other, the women were led out of the huge room first. The men waited patiently in line, their limbs and nether regions aching and heavy, but as the last female disappeared out into the corridor the big door suddenly slid shut. Confusion and panic returned with a vengeance. Some of them looked up at the silent spectators in the stands, some of them pounded their fists on the door to try and get it open again, but it was no use—they were trapped.

The neat lines of eyes stared and stared, waiting patiently for the second part of the evening's performance. The gaping, polished apertures surveyed and recorded non-stop, taking in every whimper and cry of the captives as they pottered about like dazed circus animals.

Another loud click sounded off.

Hurried, erratic reflections dashed across the lenses of the ever-watchful eyes. Warped, elongated images of steel contraptions dashed back and forth, dots of flesh landing on the shiny tips. What an encore, what a grand finale. The Spinner, The Spike, The Splitter, and The Scorcher, all in one show. How they watched and watched, silent voyeurs in the lofty shadows.

If only the thrill could last forever.

As the sound of organised barbarism rang through the innards of the ship, noises that would make the death screams from a back alley abattoir seem like the happy chirps of sparrows, the female captives were back in the dinge of the holding cell, their bodies sticky with dried sweat and semen. They'd been duped and tricked, and the grim reality of the situation was slowly sinking into their weary minds.

They were now carrying the next generation of cannon fodder, the next wave of meat to be thrown into the grinder, and they themselves had been reduced to little more than fertile livestock.

There was really only one hope, one tenuous, pitiful hope. Perhaps the Acute Ones would soon grow bored or desensitised to the slaying of *Homo sapiens*, arriving at a conclusion that slaughtering a human is no different than slaughtering a zebra or a bird. If a conclusion like that was reached, maybe they would be granted the same fate as some of the others: ejection into the unforgiving void of space, a push into oblivion.

Sitting in the darkness, their bellies set to swell from insemination, they could only hope.

BURIED MEMORY

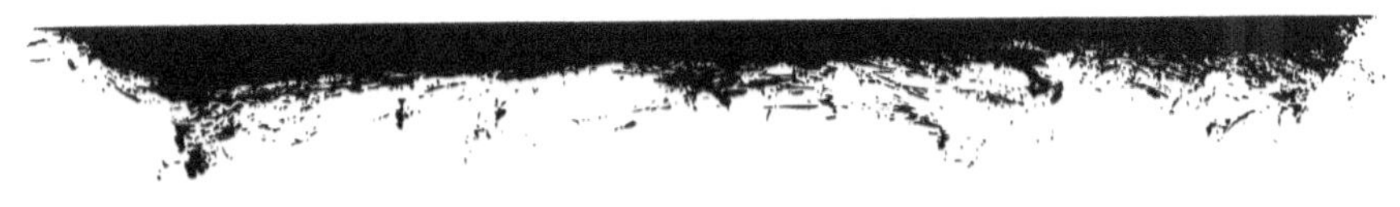

His life had gotten nasty
Too many thoughts of hurt
He paid some cash to wipe them
To throw them to the dirt

The change in him was instant
Things were nice and rosy
Until his sleep was altered
Visions dark and ghostly

Horrifying pictures
Now occupied his mind
Were they just mirages?
Or real objects to find?

Justin put on his coat and shoes and stared at his reflection in the hallway mirror for a moment. A distraught, tired man looked back out at him from the reflective pane of glass, eyes full of pain and torment. He was ready now, though, ready to start a new chapter in his life. The day had come, this was it. Taking a deep breath, he walked out the front door and started walking.

He was on his way to Piece of Mind, a controversial new company that'd opened up across town a few months ago. Piece of Mind offered a unique service for its customers: for a certain price, people could replace their memories with a new set of memories. And there were two options available for people: a Partial Replacement, and a Complete Replacement. The former involved only replacing a set of selected memories, whereas the latter involved completely replacing a person's entire memories.

There were various reasons why customers went to Piece of Mind. For some, it allowed them to move on in life after a traumatic event. For others, it was a way to live happily without regrets or a mediocre past nagging away at them. In both cases, however, the treatment was a revolutionary way to start a new life by replacing an old one, getting rid of unwanted mental baggage.

And Justin had plenty of regrets and mental baggage he wanted to get rid of. His young son had disappeared a few years ago, vanished without a trace, and shortly afterwards his wife had left him. Nobody knew what happened to his boy; he was out riding his bicycle one day and simply never returned. Abduction was the natural conclusion to take, but neither he nor the police knew for sure. The ordeal had weakened and crumbled the relationship between him and his wife shortly afterwards, and eventually she disappeared too, leaving him all alone in his anguish. But there was a limit to how much a person could take. He'd had enough heartache and misery; now he was ready to do something about it.

The Piece of Mind facility looked pleasant enough from the outside. As Justin approached it from the other side of the road, he gazed up at its white façade and smiled. The tall building represented a new start for him, an end to his torment.

The doctor was expecting him, so he didn't have to wait very long in the reception area. And that was good because the waiting area seemed to be full of other people just like himself: depressed, desperate, lonely souls who's only positive quality was a disposable income large enough to pay for some kind of treatment. After a few minutes twiddling his thumbs, he was ushered through to a rear section of the premises.

The doctor was a well-spoken, amiable man who put Justin at ease straightaway. 'You won't feel a thing,' he said. 'We'll put you to sleep, attach some special electrodes to your head, and then run our software program.'

Justin nodded pensively.

'The only bad part is that we'll have to shave off some of that nice hair.'

They both laughed as Justin ran a hand through his dark, parted hair. It was an unfortunate inconvenience, but not enough to put him off the treatment. Nowhere near, in fact.

With the pleasantries and the explanation out of the way, it was time for the operation to commence. He'd already decided that he was going to have a Partial Replacement, and he'd also already chosen his new memory implants from a digital catalogue that was emailed to him shortly after registering.

Each set of memories came from another human being, another person who sold them to the company. Usually the seller would be someone on their deathbed, someone in their final days wanting to earn a bit of money to pass on to their bereaved families to cover funeral costs and what have you, but not always. Sometimes the seller would be healthy and well, but struggling with financial difficulties. In both cases the donor's family, or the donor himself, would be advised to move to another city or district to avoid any awkward, unforeseen situations arising, such as accidentally bumping into the recipient on the street. The repercussions of such a thing happening were unknown, but it was agreed by all that it was probably worth avoiding.

Justin's new memories came from a relatively young, healthy man who was now living in a different part of the city, but this was restricted information that he didn't have access to.

Once he was comfortable on the bed in the surgical theatre, the doctor injected him with drugs and rendered him unconscious. As he was slipping away, his vision blurry and hazy, he knew that the next time he opened his eyes he would be a new man.

It was a bright, pleasant morning and Justin was pottering away in the kitchen, preparing his breakfast. It'd been several months since his operation and his life had certainly changed, although not as much as he'd hoped. The backdrop to his life had definitely altered in a radical way, with most of his past memories much easier to live with, but something still wasn't quite right.

Since the operation he'd started to experience bad dreams. These dreams ripped him from his sleep quite frequently, leaving him in a state of panic, despair, and terror. They contained many things, but in each one there was a rural theme. He always saw fields, trees, and dirt—always lots of dirt. He would march across boggy fields in these sleepy visions, cold wind slapping his face, and the last thing he would see before waking would always be an ominous-looking mound of dirt by his feet.

Shrugging it off at first, he told himself it was nothing.

But the dream persisted.

After a while he began to take notes in a small pad by his bed, and before long he had lots of details written down. Some nights he'd see a well-trodden path, other nights an empty field, but there'd always be that large mound of dirt at the end.

Sat at the breakfast table with a plate of toast and a cup of tea in front of him, Justin thought about this dream once more. *Could it be a real memory from my donor?* he thought. *Could it have been transferred to me by accident?* The doctor had told him that this occasionally happened, but it was very rare. But, rare or not, he was becoming increasingly convinced that the dream visions constituted real memories set in a real place. And, on top of this, he was even beginning to suspect that he knew where the place was. All of his notes, everything that he'd accumulated so far, told him that the dream took place over on the marshes to the north of the city. Even though the memory was not his, he could still recognise the area, and it very much resembled the marshes.

He was considering going back to Piece of Mind to complain and get rid of his new memories. Most of them were pleasant enough, but this re-occurring dream—or nightmare—was ruining them.

His curiosity wouldn't let him do that, however—not yet, anyway. He was determined to find out the meaning of the dream, hell-bent to work out what it stood for, and while he was sipping his tea at the table he decided then and there that he was going to pay a visit to the marshes.

If he looked around, maybe he'd find something.

Ryan paced up and down his plain, unfurnished living room like a trapped zoo animal, running things over in his head for the millionth time. Was he overreacting? It happened years ago, after all. *But if I remember, they might remember.*

This was ridiculous. He should've been enjoying himself, not pulling his hair out like this. Twenty thousand big ones were sitting in his bank account, and he'd just moved into a new luxury pad. Piece of Mind had paid him generously, but he just couldn't relax and enjoy his money. *This is what happens when you read the small print afterwards, you fool.*

Ryan had been in such a rush to sell his memories and earn some cash, he hadn't looked into the details thoroughly enough beforehand. In one of the booklets he'd just finished reading, it was written that on rare occasions a loose, stray memory was sometimes transferred to the recipient, an accidental addition to the specified set. This was a big problem for him because of that horrendous, fateful night all those years ago—the worst night of his life.

He'd been driving home one night after visiting a friend, cruising along the winding road that runs adjacent to the marshes. Two cans of beer were in his system; that was all. Okay, so he might have technically been over the limit, but not by much. It was week beer, as well, for crying out loud! And it wasn't even his fault. That kid on the bike had come screaming round the corner like a rocket, swerving this way and that way.

He could still see the boy's face slapping against the windscreen, still hear the crunch of the bike's frame folding under his tyres.

Panic was too mild a word to describe what he'd felt that night. He'd been shaking like a leaf, gagging and blubbering behind the wheel after skidding to a stop. It wasn't his fault, he knew it wasn't, but he also knew that the police would smell the cheap lager on his breath as soon as they turned up, and then things would have gotten really bad.

Desperate times call for desperate measures; that'd been his mantra that night, anyway. The mantra that he'd mumbled to himself whilst pulling the shovel out of the boot of the car and... No. He couldn't have done that, he just couldn't have. Could he?

Could Ryan Torres, model citizen, have dragged a boy's body into the forest by the marshes and buried it?

It'd been so out of character that he'd convinced himself it'd never happened. After a few weeks, when the police failed to turn up at his door, he simply put the whole thing behind him and resumed his former lifestyle. He went to work, paid his bills, watched TV, and pushed the entire experience away to some dusty corner of his mind.

And it'd been so deeply buried (pun not intended) that he managed to pass Piece of Mind's tests. They didn't buy just anyone's memories, you see; they only wanted suitable donors who could offer their customers nice, pleasant thoughts. Personality tests were conducted, psychological examinations, criminal background checks, etc., but Ryan had passed them all with flying colours. It was as if some inbuilt defence mechanism in his mind had concealed the memory for his sake, to preserve his mental health, to allow him to move on.

But now it was back.

The whole event was crystal clear in his mind once again, dislodged after reading the booklet, and he knew that somewhere out there, somewhere in the big city, there was another human being who could now be carrying the same incriminating memory in his or her head.

There was no way around it—he had to go back to the scene of the crime and remove the body in case the other person worked out where it was.

It was a windy day, and the trees lining the edge of the field swayed like tall, waving hands. Ryan retraced his steps from that fateful night all those years ago, trudging across the mud with a bag slung over his shoulder. He knew where he had to go; he could picture the exact area where the boy's body lay below the ground. What he wasn't entirely sure of, however, was what he was going to do once he got there. There was a shovel in his bag, and he planned on digging the corpse back up again, but after that he didn't really know.

After around twenty minutes or so he was close. Thin trees surrounded him and wet, mushy leaves squelched underfoot. The burial site was just a little bit farther down, at the foot of the short slope in front of him, and he began to edge towards it.

One step, two steps... Stop!

Someone was down there, a figure hunched over, digging away at the ground. Ryan was about to run, but the figure turned to face him. Two wide, maniacal eyes peered up at him through the tangle of trees and bushes, the frightened stare of someone caught in the middle of some despicable act. For a moment neither of them could do anything, they were both frozen still from shock, but the stand-off was broken when Ryan noticed the odd, uneven patches in the man's hair.

He had dark hair in a rough centre parting, but certain sections of it were shorter than others, like someone had attacked him with a set of hair clippers. That someone, Ryan guessed, must've been a doctor at Piece of Mind. And with this realisation, he knew that he'd inadvertently bumped into the recipient of his memories.

This was not good.

And it got worse.

Looking down towards the mound of dirt by the man's feet, Ryan could see small fragments of old bone jutting out here and there, thin white shards that'd been churned up by the edge of a pointy shovel. The man seemed to recognise who Ryan was, as well, putting two and two together.

'You!' he said, with a snarl. 'It's you!'

Caught up in a whirlwind of panic, the only thing Ryan could think of saying was: 'I don't know what you're talking about.'

'Bullshit! It's you! You're the one who buried this body!'

'Hey! I'm just taking a walk. I have no idea what you're saying.'

After a brief, tense pause, the man said: 'Deny it if you like. It doesn't matter. Piece of Mind have got your details on file, and I'll be reporting you as soon as I get out of here.'

Shit! Shit, shit, shit! thought Ryan. *This is exactly what I didn't want.*

He swiftly changed tact.

'Well, what are you doing out here, anyway? You don't look so innocent yourself.'

'What am I doing here?' said the man. 'I'm here to find out what this grave contains. I'm here to learn the truth about this dark memory you've given me. Or the dark memory I paid for,' he added, shaking his head.

Ryan was stumped. He really couldn't think of any words to talk his way out of this precarious situation. Instead he turned and started to backtrack across the muddy path, his heart racing in his chest like a thumping fist.

'You're not going to get away with this!' shouted the man, still standing by the open grave. 'Do you hear me?'

Staggering across the dirty terrain, Ryan thought hard about what he was going to do. The police would be knocking his door down within the next few days unless he could think of something, and he couldn't go to prison, he just couldn't.

Coming to a shaky halt, leaning against a pine tree for balance, he dipped his hand into his pocket and pulled out his phone. He had an idea.

Angry, thundering knocks echoed through the house, shaking the walls and doors. It'd been going on for a few minutes now, and the noise was growing louder and more ferocious with each second that passed. The letter box eventually opened on the front door, and a stern face peered in through the gap.

'Police! Police! Open up!'

There was movement upstairs, a gentle rustling as the owner panicked and stalled, trying to decide what to do.

'Open the door!'

'Okay! Okay! I'm coming,' he replied.

Putting a shaky hand on the latch, he pulled the door open and squinted at the officers through the bright morning light.

'Justin Hickey, you're under arrest for murder. Turn around and put your hands on your head.'

'What!?' screamed Justin. 'You've got the wrong man! It wasn't me, it was—'

'Just do it! Now!'

As Justin's hands were being cuffed, he closed his eyes and silently wept. His new life was turning out to be a disaster, and now this. He didn't bother protesting, didn't bother asking why they were arresting him instead of the real killer; he simply didn't have the energy. Sleep had evaded him for weeks, the macabre nightmare invading his senses every single night. Marched out the front of his house and pushed into the back of a waiting patrol car, his head hung low like a condemned man.

***

Detective Nolan stared at Justin incredulously from across the desk in the interview room. After a tense moment, he slid a photograph over to him.

'Care to explain this?' he said.

Justin looked down at the photo, and his jaw hung slack with disbelief. He saw himself standing in the woods, a pile of rotten bones by his feet. 'Look, I know who took this,' he said, running a hand through his patchy hair. 'He's trying to set me up. I can explain everything.'

'I'm all ears,' said the detective.

Justin told him everything, from Piece of Mind, to his dreams, to meeting the killer in the woods.

'Piece of Mind, eh? I've heard of that place. Swapping memories? Whatever next?'

'It's true,' stammered Justin. 'I—'

'I know it's a real place. I've heard of it. The thing is, Justin, there are just too many things working against you.'

'What? What do you mean?'

'Well, firstly, I just don't believe anyone would be stupid enough to sell their memories to Piece of Mind if they'd previously committed murder. That would just be plain stupid. Only a complete idiot would do such a thing.'

'But—'

'And,' Nolan continued, 'with the murder victim being your son, there's a clear link between you and the body.'

As the words came out of the detective's mouth, strange things happened to Justin. First his eyes grew wide, wider than they'd ever been before, then an icy feeling took over his blood, followed by the room spinning like he was sitting on some fairground ride.

'What... What did you say?'

'There's a link between you and the body, and you were caught red-handed at the scene. This is not looking good for you right now.'

'That... That was my son out there?'

'Don't try and play smart with me. I've been doing this job for too many years now. I—'

'Oh god! Oh god, no! This can't be happening!'

Nolan continued, taking no notice of what he perceived to be an emotional act. 'People go to this Piece of Mind place to feel better, right? To rid themselves of bad memories.'

Justin groaned in response, his face down on the desk.

'It doesn't take Einstein to work out what happened here, Justin. You were the one who killed your son all those years ago, then you found it hard to live with the guilt. You went to Piece of

Mind to get a new set of memories, to start again and forget, but you just couldn't escape your past. For some reason you returned to the burial site, and you were unlucky enough to get caught there.'

'No! No! That's just not true!'

'I think it is, Justin,' said the detective, gazing down at the photograph with a knowing look on his face.

'I inherited the memory from Piece of Mind!'

'Can you prove it?'

'Just go and speak to them! They'll explain everything to you!'

'I'll be paying them a visit, sure,' the detective said, albeit rather skeptically.

'And anyway, the photograph proves what I'm saying!' screamed Justin. 'How would this other guy know where the grave was unless he'd been there before?'

'You're still trying to tell me that your memory donor took this photograph?'

'Yes!'

'Can you prove that?'

'Well, no, but... Look, who do you think took it?'

'It was sent in anonymously; we don't know. We recognised you, though, due to the fiasco with your missing son a few years ago.'

'This is rubbish! The killer took it! The asshole who killed my son! And let me tell you, if I'd known at the time who he was...'

The detective was watching Justin with a pitying look, the kind of look you'd give a child who was lying very unconvincingly.

'G... Get in contact with Piece of Mind!' he cried, trying to control his breathing. 'They must have this guy's information on file.'

'Yeah, okay, we'll do that,' replied Nolan, writing down a few details on a piece of paper. 'And in the meantime, you can get some rest down in the cells.'

'You're locking me up? This is an injustice! You can't—'

'You're a murder suspect, Justin. Unless some other kind of evidence springs up from somewhere, I'm afraid you're not going anywhere.'

And with that, the detective nodded to a guard standing outside the room, and Justin was escorted to a holding cell down in the basement section of the police station.

Detective Nolan parked outside the Piece of Mind building and walked into the reception area. Looking around, he noticed five or six people sat in the room, all looking glum and desperate in their own way.

Carrying the relevant warrant required to enter the premises and obtain the restricted information needed for the case, he approached the receptionist with an air of confidence and asked to speak to the manager. A few moments later, a doctor in a long white coat took him into a back office.

'What can I do for you, Detective?'

'I need to ask you a few questions about a customer of yours.'

'Well, I'd be happy to oblige, Detective, but customer information is confidential and—'

'Here,' said Nolan, reaching into his pocket and handing over the stamped warrant. 'Will this do?'

After a quick scan of the document, the doctor nodded humbly and passed it back. 'Okay, what do you need to know?'

'I need to know about a customer called Justin Hickey.'

The doctor repeated the name and scribbled it down. 'I'll search the database and see if it's on there. Just give me a moment.'

When he returned, he was holding Justin's file. 'Is there anything in particular that you're looking for, Detective?'

'Well, firstly, what kind of treatment did he have?'

'He had a Partial Replacement, meaning only some of his memories were replaced.'

'Can you show me the exact ones which were replaced? And what they were replaced with?'

After finding the relevant section of the file, the doctor handed it over to Nolan so that he could read through it himself. The room was silent for a few minutes as he read through the pages, scanning through the descriptions of deleted memories and replacement memories. Finding nothing particularly suspicious, the detective closed the entire folder and let out a thoughtful sigh.

'Let me ask you something, Doctor. Is it true that stray, random memories sometimes get transferred by accident?'

'Unfortunately, yes. It does happen sometimes.'

'And can you see those memories? Do you have them stored on your system?'

'I'm afraid not. Stray memories bypass our system and slip straight into the recipient's head unnoticed. The only person who sees them is the recipient himself. And, of course, the donor.'

'Who *was* the donor? Who provided Justin's new memories?'

The doctor went to say something, but then hesitated. Detective Nolan, having seen this gesture many times before whilst asking people for information, knew exactly what it meant.

'This is covered by the warrant, Doctor. I'm entitled to any information I deem relevant for the case.'

'Okay, well, I could find out the donor's name if you'll excuse me again for a moment. That information will be on a separate file.'

'Sure, no problem. Take your time.'

When the doctor returned a second time, there was a very strange, apprehensive look on his face. 'I'm not quite sure what's going on here, Detective, but the man you're looking for is actually here in the building right now.'

Nolan stiffened in his seat. 'What?'

'Erm, come this way and I'll show you.'

The doctor led him out into some kind of recovery room.

'That's him?'

'Yes. His name is Ryan Torres.'

The two of them were staring down at an unconscious man spread out on a bed. A pale green gown covered his body, of the type you usually see in hospitals, and parts of his hair had been shaven off.

'He came in this morning,' said the doctor. 'We noticed that he had previously sold his memories to us, but that was no reason to refuse him treatment.'

Scratching his chin in contemplation, looking at the comatose patient lying before him, Nolan considered his options. 'So,' he said, after a while, 'what kind of treatment has Ryan Torres just had?'

Justin sat in the corner of the cell, wallowing in the semi-darkness. Sleep was still a luxury he didn't enjoy, and his face was tired, weary, and covered with several days' worth of stubble.

The various noises and bustle of the police station echoed down from above, providing a faint backdrop of muffled voices, jangling keys, and footsteps. Three times a day a set of these footsteps would grow louder as an officer brought him down a tray of food, pushing it through the bars opposite his bed, and judging by the noise that's what seemed to be happening right now. Something was wrong, though. It was mid-afternoon, and he'd eaten lunch about an hour ago. Nobody came down to the cell at this time, so who could it be?

Staring over towards the steel bars, his bloodshot eyes straining to focus through the gloom, Justin was suddenly greeted by the sight of an immaculately-dressed man in a suit. Reaching the bottom of the stairs, he placed a leather briefcase down on the ground and peered into the cell.

'Justin?'

'Y…Yes?' he replied, his voice a croaky whisper.

'Hi, I'm George Mills. Your lawyer. Nice to meet you.'

Climbing up to his feet, Justin traipsed over to the bars and shook the man's hand, taking in his sharp, pristine appearance. 'What's going on, Mr. Mills? When—'

'George. Please call me George,' he said, with a courteous smile.

'When am I getting out of this place, George?'

The lawyer looked away from Justin then, avoiding eye contact. 'That, I don't know.'

'What? What do you mean?'

'The detective in charge of your case went over to Piece of Mind recently, Justin. And…'

'And what?'

'And it was established that any stray, accidental memory you might've acquired can't be traced or proven.'

Justin groaned and slumped, hanging on to the bars for balance. 'And what about—'

'Your donor? He's been identified as a Mr. Ryan Torres. Police have searched his house, his car, his computer, and his phone, and they've found no incriminating evidence.'

'He's deleted the photo from his phone, the bastard!' screamed Justin, now pacing up and down the cell in a state. 'Let's get Piece of Mind to scan his brain! He's holding an incriminating memory in his head! The doctors over there can do that! They could find it—'

'I'm afraid that won't be possible, Justin.'

'Not possible! Not fucking possible! Why not?'

The lawyer took a very deep breath, then delivered the news as delicately as possible. 'Because Mr. Torres has had Complete Replacement surgery. All of his original memories are gone.'

'No! Nooo! This can't be happening!'

'Try to stay calm, Justin. I highly recommend that you—'

Justin snapped. He'd reached a limit of tolerance and self-composure. He threw his hands through the steel bars and grabbed the silky collar of the lawyer's suit, pulling him and yelling in his face. After a few seconds of this crazed attack, with the two of them scuffling and wrestling through the divider like wild chimpanzees, a handful of officers came hurling down the stairs with handcuffs and mace. A huge cloud of mace hit Justin square in the face, setting his skin and eyes on fire, and he released his grip on the lawyer's shirt and tumbled down to the floor. Once the lawyer was taken away to safety, Detective Nolan appeared among the group of officers and peered down at Justin as he rolled and thrashed around on the ground.

'You're really not doing yourself any favours, Mr. Hickey. You're really not.'

'You've got the wrong man! You've made a mistake!'

'Huh. If I had a pound for every time I heard that,' he mused. 'Okay, boys, let's leave him to it. Just bring him down his dinner at six o' clock.'

Everyone turned and left, walking up the concrete staircase to the offices above. A few minutes later Justin was all alone once again, the gory details of his son's death replaying over and over in his head, the images and visions becoming more lucid and clear each time around. With the mace eating away at his eyes he didn't even have the comfort of distracting himself by looking around the room; all he could do was curl up in a ball and endure the never-ending torment of his mind.

———

Ryan Torres leaned back in his seat as he drove along the winding lanes. The surgery had rendered him confused and disoriented for quite some time, but he was now adjusting to his new life. He still had plenty of money in the bank—even though he didn't really remember why—and so he was on his way to the coast to enjoy a weekend break.

An assortment of implanted memories swam around his brain as he navigated the car around the curved roads, all sweet and rosy, and things seemed very good indeed.

But then something odd happened.

A wide expanse of open land appeared over on the left-hand side of the road, a wet field with a thicket of trees further back, and for a split second it looked faintly familiar. Something about the layout of the place triggered his mind, some strange sense of deja vu, and he gazed over at the scene in mild bewilderment.

Had he been here before?

As he drove on, the moment passed, however, and he shook his head and focused back on the road. The doctor had told him that his recovery would take time and that there'd be moments of confusion like this.

Raising the volume on the radio, he put his foot down and sped off into the distance, ready for the exciting times ahead of him.

THE UNBORN

He was a junky boozer, wasting away his days
The lowest of the low, lost in a drug-fueled haze
But then he had a visit, from unexpected guests
They knew him inside out, and put him to the test

Stanley sat slouched on the torn sofa, a fog of cigarette smoke hanging lazily around his head. Opposite him, one of his cronies was gulping down the last mouthfuls of warm, flat beer from a can.

'We're out of drink,' he said, crushing the empty can in his hand and then throwing it down onto an empty crate by their feet.

'Who's turn is it then?' came another voice from the kitchen.

The question caused a tense silence to hang in the air for a moment, but then Stanley felt all eyes upon him as his two friends faced his way, one from the sofa opposite him and one from the doorway of the kitchen. He didn't bother putting up a fight, for he knew fair well that it was his turn to walk round to the late-night off-licence to do a beer run. Closing his bloodshot eyes he sighed in submission, accepting the fact that this arduous duty had to be carried out.

Beer-run duty was inconvenient, but not because he had to spend any money; it was inconvenient because it involved walking into the store, picking up a crate of beer, and then pelting out of the door as fast as his legs could carry him, hoping that the shop owner wouldn't bother taking chase.

'Come on, Stanley boy, get your jacket on,' said his wide-eyed acquaintance from the kitchen doorway, with a shark-like grin spread across his face.

'All right, all right,' muttered Stanley, climbing to his feet and kicking his way through the cigarette butts, cans, and takeaway boxes that littered the carpet.

'You can even have a livener before you go. How about that?' called the voice from the kitchen, amidst the sound of a card tapping against a glass surface.

Walking past his semi-conscious friend on the sofa, he entered the kitchen where he was passed a rolled-up bank note.

With his nostrils still stinging, Stanley marched down the road towards the late-night shop with an edgy spring in his step. He was particularly anxious tonight for two reasons: firstly, he'd done so many beers runs from this area that the shopkeepers now knew his face, making his job twice as risky. Secondly, the last time he'd walked under the flyover that he was now approaching, he'd ended up in a nasty confrontation with a crazed homeless man who'd jumped out at him from the shadows, grabbing him by the scruff of the neck.

It'd happened a week ago. He'd been heading over to his friend's squat with a stolen laptop late in the evening, and as he was passing under the bridge in the dark, a crazed, grotty-looking, hooded man pounced on him from the shadows, blocking his path. His initial thought was that the man's intention was to rob him of the laptop, but it soon became clear that that wasn't the case. Instead, he'd seemed hell-bent on having a drunken rant, yapping on about something that didn't even seem to make any sense.

'What the fuck are you doing?' Stanley had yelled, as the man's knuckles pushed against his neck and chest.

With his face completely hidden in shadow, the voice that seeped out from beneath the hood had been grave and intense.

'I'll give you one week to turn your life around. One week to start appreciating what you've got.'

Half choking, Stanley replied, 'What the hell are you on, you freak?! Get off me!'

'One week,' said the voice from the shadows. 'No more.'

If it hadn't been for the fact that he'd had a laptop computer in his hand and fifty quid waiting for him down the road, he would've swung for him, but he'd been more keen to sell his stolen goods at the time than stand there with some nutcase. Later that night, after several beers and lines of cocaine, he'd forgotten all about that little encounter, but now, as the flyover came into sight just up ahead of him, it all came flooding back. With no other way to get to the off-licence he had no choice but to follow the same path, so he walked down into the shadowy, urine-stained recesses of the underpass once again, his head turning at every sound.

Despite feeling tense, jumpy, and jittery all the way through, he made it out of the underpass unapproached and so now turned his attention to the bigger task at hand: stealing the alcohol. The bright lights of the shop sign beckoned him from over in the distance, and as he crossed the road towards the store he braced himself for action.

The plan went as well as it could have. He picked up the drink, headed for the tills, then, at the last minute, as the shopkeeper had been occupied with another customer, he'd drifted over to the door and slipped out without paying. He'd made it a safe distance away by the time the angry shop owner had come running out the front of the store, and despite his angry yells and fist waving he hadn't even bothered chasing after him.

The job was done but he knew that he had to keep on moving, so with a hand on each side of the crate he retraced his steps back towards his friend's squat where thirsty mouths needed watering. Knowing that he now had another good few hours of drinking ahead of him, as well as having the comforting knowledge that it'd be another couple of days before the next theft was expected of him, he was in high spirits. But this all changed as he passed under the flyover for the second time, for as he stepped through the damp shadows he felt a steely grip clamp around his throat. He was thrown back against one of the concrete pillars and the entire case of beer fell from his hands, cans bursting and fizzing-up all over the pavement.

'What are you doing? Get off me, you f—'

'I'm disappointed, Stanley. I really am.'

'You freak! Get your hand off my neck!'

He lashed out at the man but his lean build was deceiving, his strength unfaltering and relentless.

'You've had so many chances, so many opportunities.'

'I haven't got time for any more of your ramblings! Get...' Stanley paused, as if noticing something. 'Hey! How do you know my name? Who are you?' He squinted, trying desperately to see who was inside the shadowy pit of the hood, but could see nothing except the faint bridge of the man's nose.

'I know more about you than you know about yourself.'

'If you want the beers just take them,' spat Stanley.

A gruff noise emanated from within the hood.

'Huh. So I can proceed to become you? Drinking away my life and wasting away my days? If only I had the chance...'

Movement caught Stanley's eye from across the road as a man walked by. He panicked, thinking for a moment that it may have been the shopkeeper, but it wasn't him. He did, however, look vaguely familiar, and for a good few seconds Stanley couldn't pull his eyes away from this passing pedestrian despite the hooded vagrant continuing to rough him up.

'Are you listening to me?' raged the tramp. 'I said, if only I had the chance!'

'What do you want?' said Stanley, turning his head back towards him.

'I wanted to see you turn yourself around, to realise what potential you've got, to realise your amazing luck and good fortune. I wanted to see you achieve something, something that would've alleviated my own pain and torment.'

'You're bloody loopy! Get off of me!'

He was just about to raise a knee to the man's groin and shake himself free when another pedestrian came walking by, this time a woman on the same side of the road. Just a few feet away, she turned her head mockingly towards him, and once again Stanley saw something remarkably familiar in this stranger's features. The curve of her nose, the width of her chin, the cheekbones...

'But it's too late now, you've blown it!' the attacker continued.

'Look, what is this?'

There was a stony silence for a few seconds, during which Stanley could only lean back against the pillar and look helplessly towards the faint outline of a face before him.

'Did you know that the amount of sperm cells a man creates over the course of a lifetime adds up literally to the hundreds of billions?'

'What?'

'On the night of your conception alone,' continued the man, 'you were in competition with up to one billion other sperm cells. That's one billion potential lives—'

'What are you? Are you a junkie, or some kind of preacher?'

'...one billion potential lives, people who could've become artists, scientists, doctors, engineers, astronauts or writers.' The hood leaned in closer, so close that Stanley could now see two thin, glistening eyes staring out at him. 'But you know what, Stanley? Those people didn't make it into existence. You beat them here; you took the life that they were all competing for. So tell me: what exactly have you done with it?'

The man was now so close to him that the mist of his breath was merging with his, and the wide brim of his hood was touching his forehead.

'I don't have to explain myself to you! Get the fuck off me! Who do you think you are?'

It was then, whilst maintaining an iron grip on his neck, that the man pulled back his baggy hood and revealed himself. For Stanley, it was like looking in the mirror.

'I'm one of the many who didn't make it, Stanley. One of the many who was beaten before life even began, one of the many who could've grown into something great, something legendary.'

Stunned into a paralysing silence, Stanley could do nothing but study the man's face. His prominent nose, pointed ears, crooked teeth, and dishevelled hair gave such a strong resemblance to his own, it looked like the man had stolen his own features. Looking at this replica of himself, he wondered whether he might've simply bumped into a long-lost brother, or a troubled relative who'd tracked him down online. The tingling feeling in his gut, however, was telling him a different story.

The two of them were now causing a scene, and clusters of passersby were stopping to see what the commotion was. With the damaged beer cans rolling and leaking by his feet, Stanley was reminded that he was still too close to the off-licence for comfort and so made a fresh attempt to shake himself free and scarper.

'Enough of this shit!' he shouted, straining and turning against the hand on his neck. 'If you want to rant and ramble on all night, crawl back to your cardboard box and rant to yourself, because I haven't got time for it!'

A wry grin formed across the man's face, causing his eyes and teeth to glisten from the glow of a distant streetlight. 'Fine, I'll let you go, but it's not just me you have to answer to.' With one last surge of strength, the man yanked his collar and brought his face even closer. 'Like I said, there was one billion people who never made it.'

Pushed aside and now free from the man's grip, Stanley straightened himself and edged away from him. Most of the beers were ruined so he didn't even bother picking up the crate; instead he began to turn and head back to the squat emptyhanded. But what he saw all around him stopped him in his tracks, causing him to pause in disbelief. The pockets of people across the road had grown in number, and were now all staring unashamedly at him. And there were more approaching, too, from both sides of the road. Figures were appearing all around him, lining the pavements, stood on the road crossings, and drifting across the patches of grass in the middle distance. Eyes peered out from behind bus stops, heads turned in passing cars, ashen faces looked up from wooden benches, and up above the flyover rows of onlookers were leaning over the rail casting their hateful, fiery glances down towards where he stood. But it wasn't just the vast numbers that scared him, it was the faces themselves, the similar, replicated, homogeneous faces that all looked related, regardless of whether they were male or female. As the crowds continued to advance he slowly retreated, and the hooded man finally called out his parting words.

'Don't ever say you didn't have a chance.'

As these grave words were sinking in, a deep murmur echoed through the streets, an ominous growl that spoke of an impending doom. This low, rumbling, earthy noise made the tarmac underneath his feet vibrate, causing his balance to falter. It was then that he saw movement on the horizon, a giant slither flowing down the curve of the main road. A flux of bodies, a gargantuan crowd, all advancing down towards him like a billion-strong army with hearts full of rage.

His casual retreat turned into an all-out sprint in the opposite direction as the behemoth mob came towards him, a human tidal wave consuming the nighttime streets. The thunder and roar grew louder and louder, however, no matter how fast he ran, and before long he began to feel the brush of hands against his coat sleeves and sharp tugs at his collar. An endless stream of silhouettes emerged from every surrounding side street and alleyway; more yells, more tugs, more screams from over his shoulder, then a swiping kick to his ankle sent him stumbling and staggering to the curbside. A futile attempt was made to shield himself from the onslaught of kicks and punches raining down from above, but with too many fists to count let alone defend himself from he resorted to curling up into a ball, regressing back into the fetal position as the life he'd been granted came to a harsh, painful end.

A DATE WITH DEATH

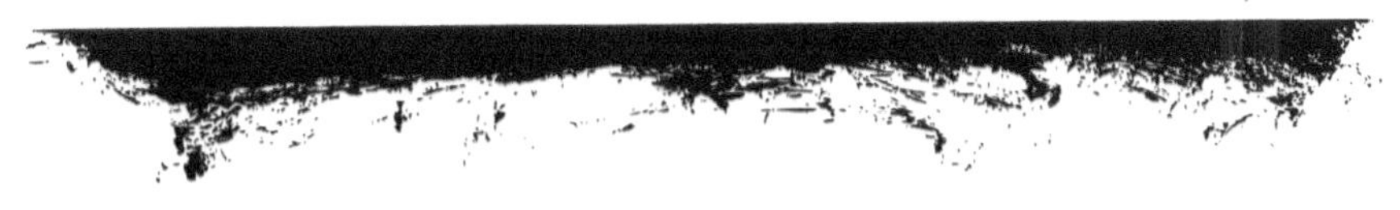

He goes by the name of Dillon
Some would say he's a villain
If you want someone dead
Without leaving your bed
There's no better person to see

He deals in death dates
At affordable rates
Earthquake, or a fire
Whatever you desire
Your foe will no longer be

No risk of jail time
It's the perfect street crime
You hand over some cash
Learn the date of a crash
And saunter away scot free

A thick stream of traffic roared by on the motorway down below, saloons and hatchbacks screaming along the asphalt. On the roof of an adjacent building, sitting calmly in one of the plastic sun-chairs of a rooftop bar with a notepad and pen in his hand, Dillon could see it all: a thousand glistening cars zipping by like fireflies under the afternoon sun, bonnets and windshields reflecting the warm, yellow glare. On the other side of the road, across the vast expanse of tarmac and concrete barriers, a line of multi-story hotels stretched off in either direction, high-rise buildings filled with spas, swimming pools, and luxury rooms that were sure to put a dent in anyone's wallet. Figures lined the balconies of some of these complexes, dots of people watching the busy freeway down below from the comfort of their rented rooms. Dillon glanced down at his watch again, then back over towards one of the opposite buildings. It would happen any minute now; he knew it would. Leaning back in his chair, taking the cap off his pen, a wry grin spread across his face.

The building was about fifty metres away, but he still felt the blast—a shock wave vibrating through the air like bass from a giant speaker. Smoke rose up from within the structure, followed by flames, hotel guests trapped several stories up with no way out other than leaping over the edge of one of the balconies. Dillon felt a wave of guilt as he watched the hotel burn. As people rose from their seats around him, shouting and screaming at the sight of this horrible tragedy, he hardly batted an eyelid. He was used to watching pain and suffering now, and it was possible to become numbed and desensitized to anything if you saw enough of it. Watching disasters like this had become a business for him, and he couldn't let emotions get in the way of money. As the building continued to crumble, he shrugged off this pang of guilt, then made a note of the exact time and second that the structure's foundations collapsed.

Dillon saw himself as a kind of hitman, or an exterminator of sorts. People came to him when they wanted someone gone, and as long as he was satisfied that they deserved it he always made sure that it happened. The real paradox of it all, though, was that Dillon had never actually killed anyone in his life.

It all started a few years back when he'd cracked the problem of time travel. Working alone in his lockup, researching, building, and fine-tuning, he'd managed to achieve what the professionals had been striving for for decades: a fully functioning, fully programmable time machine. If it'd been anyone else, they would've been rich from it, patenting the design and raking in millions overnight. But Dillon had far too many enemies to be able to enjoy a success story like that, and the enemies on his list included the authorities themselves. He was a smart guy and always had been, but he wasn't so good at playing his cards right. He could've been a top scientist if he'd put his mind to it back in the day, but instead he'd slipped into a life of fraudulent, petty crime, fleecing large corporations of their money in a variety of unlawful but genius ways.

So he was unable to cash in on his invention the legal way, but that was okay, as he'd come up with his own unique method of generating money from it. With the help of his contraption, Dillon was in the extermination business. The concept was simple: he'd travel a few months or years into the future, look in the papers and on the news for reports of traffic accidents, terrorist attacks, natural disasters or disease outbreaks, make a note of all of the dates and times, then travel back to the present day armed with a notepad full of what he liked to call: "disaster dates." Occasionally, as like today, he might even travel to these disasters to witness them firsthand, getting a more accurate time, writing down the exact second of impact, explosion, ignition or detonation, etc., etc.

People came to him with fistfuls of cash, unhappy and disgruntled about some rival who'd wronged them, some spouse who'd cheated on them, or some waster who'd caused them a certain amount of grief. Dillon had standards, however. He wouldn't sell dates to any Tom, Dick, or Harry who'd had a falling-out with someone; he'd always talk to his clients first, gauging whether the victim in question truly deserved to die or not. He liked to think of his work as a kind of cleansing of society, weeding out the unworthy and exterminating those who were a stain on humanity. Customers wanting a disaster date to settle some petty feud would sometimes be turned away, but if a victim of some heinous crime turned up wanting to seek the justice that the authorities wouldn't or couldn't provide, he'd always sell them a date. This moral standard of his helped him sleep at night.

Luring people into places where an accident was due to happen was no easy task. It was tricky and unpredictable, and sometimes his customers failed. This was ultimately the customer's problem, of course, not Dillon's. Once the date's sold, it's up to the customer to set their enemy up and lure them into their traps; Dillon was merely a merchant selling a date, or a date merchant. If a pile-up on a main stretch of motorway was due to take place at 15.37pm on a Tuesday afternoon, for example, and their target arrived a minute earlier and escaped it all unscathed, it would mean they would have to purchase another date and try to lure their enemy into a different trap. This was all an added bonus for Dillon, though, who would simply end up earning more money from the whole affair.

There was really no better way of putting it: Dillon had created a way for people to get away with murder. If a person died in a random pile-up on the freeway, no detective or constable would get suspicious; if a recently acquitted rapist was unlucky enough to drown on a commercial boat-cruiser that accidentally sailed into a storm, no officer from the murder investigation unit was going to launch an inquiry.

Rising from the sun-chair, turning away from the rectangular fireball on the other side of the motorway, Dillon made his way to the stairs. The news stations would later put the hotel fire down to a gas leak, a faulty oven, or a cracked pipe somewhere down in the basement. Whatever it was, it would certainly provide one of his customers with a way to rid themselves of a nuisance, he thought, as he made for the exit.

As the screaming wails of several fire engines rose up from somewhere in the distance, Dillon walked back to the site where he'd parked his precious machine, satisfied that this particular disaster date was accurate and true.

It's rare for customers to have more than one target, but not unheard of. It happened occasionally, but only when someone landed themselves in some kind of deep trouble or didn't cover their tracks properly. When Dillon received a call on his business phone one afternoon, up to his neck in grease and spanners whilst maintaining his machine, he should've known that this was one of those people. The voice coming over the line was panicked and nervous, laced with fear.

'Oh, er, hi. I'm looking for a...a date,' he said.

Suppressing an immature urge to tell the man that he wasn't running a dating agency, Dillon replied, 'Who gave you my number?'

'Err, an old customer of yours. Look, don't worry, you can trust me. I'm just after one of these future dates. Could I...get one?'

Dillon sighed and looked at his watch. He wasn't planning on doing business today, especially with a random caller, but it'd been a while since he'd sold a date, and he knew the money would come in handy.

'Can you get to Thrifton Pier by six o' clock?' he said, eventually.

'Yeah, sure.'

'What's your alias?'

Caught off guard for a second, the man hesitated, then, 'Call me Jack. What about you?'

'Bill. My name's Bill.'

'Okay.'

After discussing the financial side of things, Dillon finished with, 'See you at six o' clock. And bring cash.'

Meeting people at his lockup was too risky; he always met customers elsewhere. This was a safety precaution that he'd been practising ever since his unique business had been up and running, and it prevented a lot of bother. The location of his machine was top secret, so he couldn't risk letting anyone come near the small garage in which it sat. The machine had been built and assembled within the confines of the garage's brick walls, and to this day Dillon was the only person to have ever laid eyes on the bizarre structure. Its mechanical complexity was completely hidden from the rest of the world, the cylinders, cogs, and coils of its chunky body nonexistent to everyone except him. This was a shame, really. A waste. Even so, Dillon didn't plan on changing things anytime soon.

There was still a lot of odd jobs he needed to do to the machine this evening, so when he left to go and meet the customer he left his tools out on the floor and locked the shutter door. Once outside, he made his way over to his car, notepad in hand.

The pier was empty when he arrived to meet his new client, so he sat himself down on one of the many wooden benches overlooking the river, the afternoon sun bouncing off the water in golden slivers. He was lost in this pleasant riverside view when he felt the bench move and creak as a second person came and sat down next to him. Turning his head, he saw the face of a tired, distraught-looking man, a man who obviously had not slept for several days.

'Bill?' he said, shakily.

'Yes. You must be Jack?'

'Yes. It's so good to meet you at last. Look, I...I desperately need one of these dates.'

Dillon never had any qualms about asking his customers why they wanted somebody eliminated. He was always very aware of the severity of his trade, acknowledging that every date sold was essentially someone's death sentence, and so, calmly and candidly, without any hesitation, he asked the man why he was so eager to get his hands on one of his dates.

'It's my sister,' he replied, looking down at the floor. 'She's in danger. She has a fiancé who's bad news. He belongs to some traveller family that's renowned for causing trouble around town.'

It was easy to sympathise with Jack. He was a small man, lean and skinny, with a timidness about him. He wanted to stick up for his sister, but he didn't have the physical power to do so.

'Does he really deserve to die, though?' asked Dillon, with a questioning frown.

'I've no other choice! I can't bear to see her get beaten again! I—'

'He hits her?'

'Yes! I've lost count of how many times.'

'Well, I wouldn't usually sell a date to someone just so that they can settle a family feud, but you look pretty shaken up about this.'

'I am! Believe me, I am!'

'So, what kind of date do you want?'

'Well... Wh... What have you got?'

'I've got car pile-ups, train derailments, sunken boats, terrorist attacks, fires—'

'Err, I'll have a car pile-up, please.'

'Sure.'

Dillon pulled out his notebook and started flipping through pages, scanning long lists of times, dates, and locations.

'Okay, are you ready for this?'

'Yes,' said Jack, holding his phone so he could type in the details.

'Ten twenty-three a.m. on the twenty-third of August,' Dillon whispered. 'The slip road at junction twenty-three on the M72 northbound. Twelve car pile-up, numerous fatalities.'

'T...Thanks,' said Jack, tapping away at his phone.

'Got the money?'

'Yes, of course. Here...'

A thick wad of notes changed hands across the bench, then Dillon rose to his feet. He took one last look at the pitiful man, then turned and headed back across the pier.

A newspaper stand in the corner of the library displayed a selection of tabloid headlines, and Dillon took two from the rack and then went and sat down. There was a variety of different ways in which one could collect disaster dates, and sometimes, out of a desire for ease and convenience, he simply resorted to visiting newsagents and libraries to skim through the papers. It wasn't the most exciting of methods, but it often did the trick. Customers seldom wanted to wait longer than a few weeks or months to rid themselves of a nuisance, so there was no real need to travel long distances through time.

So, nestled in amongst the long rows of books in the public library, he made himself comfy and flicked through the newspapers. A fatal plane hijacking caught his eye, and he made a note of the details, recognising the value of such a fail-safe date. Unlike a car pile-up or an earthquake, where a target had to be in exactly the right place at the right time—or wrong place at the wrong time, depending on how you looked at it—for it to work, a disaster date involving a plane would guarantee the death of the target as long as they could be tricked or persuaded into boarding the plane. The same went for boat accidents, or building fires.

Moving on, the next thing that got his attention was an article about a bus that'd tipped over on a roundabout in some suburban town, killing several passengers. He wrote down the bus route and the name of the street, along with the other details, then continued to browse.

Within thirty minutes another page of his notepad was filled with new disaster dates—precious information that could be exchanged for cash. He put the newspapers back on the rack, left the library, then walked nervously out into the bustle of the street outside.

Dillon could never truly relax whilst collecting dates, as he always had to leave his machine stashed away somewhere. He had a few favourite places, which he considered to be safe, but there was always the nagging worry that it'd be discovered by a group of teenagers or a random dog-walker, which could cause all kinds of problems. One of his preferred spots was a large nature reserve a couple of miles east of the city centre, well away from the traffic and the crowds. The place was packed full of thick foliage and head-high brambles, ideal for arriving and departing unseen, but it was never completely risk free.

It was this nature reserve that he was heading to now, rushing along, eager to get back to the present day. After walking for thirty minutes, he finally got there, breathing a sigh of relief at the sight of the shiny pipes, pistons, valves, and cylinders that were nestled in a juxtaposition among the wild greenery where he'd left it. Climbing over the nettles and kicking his way through the vines, Dillon climbed into the seat of his finely tuned mechanism, the chrome walls encircling him from either side. Travelling back to the present day was far less challenging than travelling to the future, because all he really had to do was set the coordinates for his garage and he could arrive without any risk of being seen. He'd travelled in his machine dozens of times now, but it never got any less thrilling or spectacular. His whole entire body would tingle with a sense of weightlessness as the fabric of space and time was broken, followed by a nauseating visual display of flashing kaleidoscope colours as his blood rushed relentlessly around his head. It could, at times, be quite an enjoyable experience, but he was usually relieved once it was over.

And this time was no different. When everything felt still and stable again, he opened the door of the machine and gazed around at the inside of his storage lockup, his head still spinning from the inter-dimensional roller-coaster ride he'd just endured. Satisfied that another day's work was completed, he spent a few minutes shutting down the machine and tidying things away before heading home. Opening the garage door to get out, however, he was confronted with a sight that he didn't expect to see.

Lingering a few feet away from the door, a figure stood facing him, shoulders hunched underneath a heavy coat. Dillon quickly stepped out and slammed the door shut behind him, hoping that whoever it was didn't get a glimpse of his contraption. He felt quite flushed and panicked at the presence of this unwanted stranger, but when they took a couple of steps towards him into the light, his panic turned to anger.

'What the hell are you doing here?' he growled, recognising the tired face of Jack, the guy he'd met at the pier a couple of weeks ago.

'Is this where it's kept?' he asked, looking across the steel shutters for any gaps that he could see through.

'How the hell did you find me? You're not supposed to be here!'

'It doesn't matter, I—'

'Yes, it does matter! Nobody's supposed to come here!'

'Don't worry, I—'

'How did you find me?'

'Oh, okay,' sighed Jack. 'I followed you here from the pier the other week. I just...I just wanted to see this thing with my own eyes.'

'Well, I don't care what you want. You need to get out of here, now!'

'I mean, I didn't believe it at first. I thought it was all rumour and tales. But that date you sold me...it...it really worked.'

Dillon took a moment to secure the padlock on the shutter door, then turned back around and squared up to Jack.

'You're taking liberties, do you know that? You got what you wanted, so now leave me alone.'

'I'm sorry, but I need another date,' he said, squirming under Dillon's steely gaze.

'Another date? What's the matter now?'

'My...My brother-in-law's death has upset someone, and I need a second date to...erm, you know, tie up a loose end.'

Dillon wanted nothing more than to get this man away from his lockup, away from his machine, and if that meant selling him another date then so be it, he thought. Dipping his hand into his pocket, he pulled out his notepad—which was full of new dates.

'I'm not sure about a plane hijacking,' Jack said. 'It's a bit too large-scale.'

'What about a bus accident, then?'

'Yes,' Jack said, after a moment's thought. 'I could pull that off.'

Times, dates, and money were exchanged between the two of them as they stood outside the row of rented garages, with Dillon looking nervously around.

'Now get the hell out of here,' he said, pocketing another wad of money. 'And don't tell anyone about this place.'

'Don't worry, I won't,' grumbled Jack, turning on his heel.

As Jack was walking away, Dillon went over to his car and climbed in. He was trembling with a mixture of rage and panic, and he felt like screaming at the top of his lungs. Nobody had ever found out about his lockup before, but now this stupid little man had discovered it. This was a game changer, a serious slip-up, and something had to be done about it.

If someone has info on you, you ought to have info on them, Dillon thought, as he considered his options.

Starting the engine, he put the car in gear and pulled out of his parking space, tailing the man at a safe distance. *If that idiot can follow me, I can follow him.*

Jack was sitting alone in his small apartment, staring at the TV as it flashed and flickered over the living room. He was a wreck; his body was tense, and his hands were shaking on his lap. He'd gone way above his head, and he knew it. He wasn't a criminal, let alone a murderer, yet he was now responsible for the deaths of two people. He'd never really believed that it was going to work, but it did, and now there was no going back. It'd taken an exhausting amount of planning, scheming and organising to get his two targets where he wanted them to be, but somehow he'd managed to pull it all off.

The first one he'd watched on the news. After getting his sister's violent fiancé to agree to meet him at a restaurant near to where the impact site was, he'd stayed at home and watched the news channels for reports on a motorway crash. To his shock and horror, several channels actually began to broadcast bulletins of a large accident that fell in line with the disaster date that he'd purchased, confirming that the date was genuine—and that he was now technically a murderer.

But even with the psychotic brother-in-law out of the way, his troubles had been far from over. The man had come from a large, close-knit family, and one of his boisterous brothers appeared shortly after the murder, asking questions and making certain implications. The pressure was on, and before long, he had a second problem on his hands, which required a second date to get rid of it. The second date was genuine, too, and the killing also went well, but the realisation that he'd now killed two people was bearing down hard on poor Jack, losing him sleep and putting his nerves constantly on edge.

Indeed, the sheer enormity of what he'd done nagged away at him day and night, and every time he ventured outside he fully expected to feel a tap on his shoulder followed by the cold snap of handcuffs, and every time the sound of police sirens echoed along the street outside, his first thought was that they must be for him. His only comfort, which he clung to dearly, was the fact that the killings were completely unprovable, and that even if somebody could prove that both men were on their way to meet him before they died, no reasonable jury would consider him guilty based on the random nature of the accidents. Jack reminded himself of this fact repeatedly in an effort to calm himself down, but still, there was a deep-set fear within him that he couldn't quite shake off.

Getting up to his feet, he walked through to the kitchen to make himself a drink. A glass of whisky would help soothe his anxiety, he decided, and he eagerly reached for the bottle of malt on his shelf. He'd hardly finished unscrewing the lid, however, when the banging started on the front door.

'Open up! We know you're in there!'

Jack stood frozen on the spot, the big glass bottle of whisky dangling from his trembling hand. He put the bottle down on the kitchen side as quietly as he could, then tiptoed back into the living room to lower the volume on the TV. A million thoughts ran through his panicked mind as he tried to identify the loud voices outside the door, but he couldn't focus on any of them. The banging and shouting continued, growing louder and angrier by the second, and just as Jack felt as though he was on the brink of a meltdown, he thought he recognised one of the voices.

'I'm telling you now, you'd better open this bloody door, or I'll...'

Yes, he knew that voice. It was one of the uncles. One of the uncles who belonged to that wretched family.

Maybe he spotted me, Jack thought.

Over the last couple of weeks, Jack had walked around here and there, passing the houses and caravans where certain members of this family lived. He didn't know why, really; he simply wanted to gauge how much trouble the two deaths had stirred up.

Another loud thump rattled the doorframe and its hinges.

'If you don't open up, I'm gonna knock the bloody door down.'

Whether the man had spotted him loitering around outside his home, or whether he'd simply used his head and linked the deaths to him by association, Jack didn't know, but either way, he wasn't going to open the door to these monsters. He started to wonder whether he could make the jump from his second-floor balcony to the pavement outside. The idea never came to fruition, however, because before he could even begin to get himself over to the window the front door came crunching down amidst a cloud of splintered wood and dust. A towering bulk of muscle filled the shattered doorway, flanked by two other figures. The floorboards creaked as the men stormed in, and Jack had nowhere to hide. The biggest of the trio advanced towards him and grabbed him by the front of his collar, lifting him high up against the wall. His wide, stubbled face completely filled Jack's field of vision.

'How did you do it?' the man said, his fist pushing tight against his chest and neck.

'Wh... What?'

'Don't play dumb with me! What's going on?! Two members of my family have died over the course of one month, and they were both on their way to meet you.'

Jack knew that this fact was indisputable, the connection too hard to ignore, but he tried to use the impossibility of the situation to his advantage.

'But how...how could it have anything to do with me? They both died in random road accidents, for crying out loud! One on a bus, and the other one in a mass pile-up on the motorway!'

A knowing look then flashed across the grisly face before him, a look that told him he wasn't going to get off the hook that easily.

'We think you've been using that...dealer.'

'Dealer?'

'You know who I mean! The date merchant. The man with the machine that everyone keeps hearing about.'

They know about the machine, too, Jack thought, feeling all hope vanishing away into nothingness. But still, backed into a corner as he was, physically and figuratively, he couldn't openly admit his involvement.

'I don't know what you're talking about,' he muttered.

The man's eyes narrowed, his jaw setting tighter.

'Well, maybe this'll get you thinking straight,' he said, before landing a gut-wrenching punch to Jack's abdomen.

The force of the blow winded him instantly, making the room spin and his stomach scream out in pain. He couldn't breathe or see through the stars that swirled before him, and as the three men moved in closer, he was barely able to hear their threatening ultimatum.

'Either you take us to this man and his machine, or your life as you currently know it ends here.'

Jack looked around at the blurred, bulky forms of the men as he gasped for air. Then, in the manner of a defeated man resigned to his fate, his head drooped down towards the floor.

Dillon paced around inside his garage, the floor scattered with tools and oily cloths. Another servicing session was over, and he was busy tidying up. Servicing the machine took longer today than it usually did. That man turning up here the other day had rattled him, and he didn't like it at all. If he started mouthing off to people about the whereabouts of his contraption, it would simply be a matter of time before the police turned up at his door. It was very doubtful that the authorities would ever be able to convict him of murder, but they would definitely try to convict him of something, and the shoeboxes full of money that he had stashed under his bed would surely aid them in that process.

And what would they make of the actual machine itself? The arrangement of chrome pipes, gears, levers, steel panels, digital displays, buttons, and handles sat in the corner like a piece of wizard engineering—what would their reaction be to it? Would they want to know where every piece of copper wire came from? Every sheet of aluminum and steel? Every computer monitor? He certainly hoped not, otherwise he could add theft to the list of offences they could incarcerate him for.

There were times when he wondered how far he could actually take his business, how long he could do it for. There was no grand plan in place, no long-term business model; he was just raking in cash week by week, building himself a nest. There would eventually come a time when he would have to put the machine out of action, maybe once he'd earned enough money to comfortably retire, but the thought of scrapping or dismantling it wasn't very appealing. Every square inch of his invention had been sweated over and laboured upon for hours, every circuit board soldered diligently, every internal computer programmed to perfection. Too much work had gone into it for him to simply disregard it like a used toy. *Maybe I could keep it here forever*, he thought, dwelling on its sentimental value.

But, as he packed away the last of his tools, preparing himself to go home, Dillon resigned himself to the fact that he would have to find another lockup now, another garage in another secret location that nobody knew about. Then, after that, he'd have to become more careful and diligent about his actions, more mindful of being watched and followed. He was busy pondering this prospect as he searched for his keys, calculating the logistical scale of such a task, when a loud rap on the shutters behind him caused him to jump and turn.

'Open up!'

Shit! Shit, shit, shit! They've found me already! thought Dillon, as the steel shutter rattled and shook against its runner.

Luckily, out of habit, he always locked himself in the garage from the inside, so he had at least a couple of minutes to think.

'Open up, or I'll kick my way through!' came the voice again, from outside.

He was trapped within the confines of his garage-space, with no way out other than the shutter door. He could hear several footsteps and voices out there, and in all probability, it was some kind of police unit. There was no way around it: he would have to unbolt the door. Nevertheless, he took his time in doing so, creating a few false alibis in his head whilst pretending to fumble around for the right key, bracing himself for the heavy questioning that was bound to happen in some interview room.

'Come on! Open up!'

'Okay. I'm opening the door now.'

As soon as Dillon opened the door and saw the three men stood before him, he knew that his first assumptions had been wrong. These were not police officers knocking on his door; this was much worse than that—they were gangsters. Police officers had to play by the rules; gangsters, on the other hand, didn't. This fact was swiftly proven when he was thrown down to the ground by the biggest man of the three, sliding a few feet across the floor from the sheer force of one of his heavy paws. The three men loomed over him like giant monuments, and behind them, over by the door, Dillon detected the presence of someone else.

'Will you get in here and shut that bloody door?' hissed one of the men, turning his head towards the small figure that was lurking in the background.

A sharp scowl spread across Dillon's face as he saw Jack stumble into his garage.

'I'm...I'm sorry! I had no choice!' trembled Jack.

Dillon wanted to get up and throttle him. The anger that he was feeling was so immense he was beginning to shake, but before he could even think about doing anything the huge man before him nodded his head towards the corner of the room.

'This is it then, I presume? This is the great machine I've heard so much about?'

Dillon nodded reluctantly, his narrowed, angry eyes still focused on Jack.

'The machine that killed two members of my family,' the man continued.

Something clicked in Dillon's head, then. Suddenly, he knew exactly who these people were.

'Search him,' said the big man, to the other two flanking his sides. 'Empty his pockets.'

'Look, I'm not responsible for the deaths of your relatives,' Dillon cried, as all of his pockets were turned over. 'And neither is my machine. I just sell dates to people who ask for them. I don't get involved in anything after that.'

Jack was wincing and squirming in the corner at this, but Dillon didn't give a damn.

'Maybe you've got a point,' said the man, shooting a brief cold stare over in Jack's direction. 'And that's why I'm not here for revenge, exactly. I'm here for the machine.'

His two sidekicks then handed him the contents of Dillon's pockets, which amounted to his phone, wallet, and keys. Opening the wallet, he started pulling out bankcards and driving licences, searching for a name.

'The thing is, though...' He squinted down at one of the cards. '...Dillon. How do I know that this thing's real and safe to use?'

One of the sidekicks piped up when he heard this.

'It's obviously real! That piece of shit over there used it to kill—'

'We don't know that yet! He could've had them killed another way!'

'It's real,' blurted Dillon. 'I assure you.'

'That may be true, but I ain't gettin' in it until I see some kind of evidence.'

'Let's get him to turn it on,' said the sidekick. 'He can get into it himself.'

'Nobody's switchin' that bloody thing on until we know a bit more about it!'

Dillon was watching the big man closely as he said this, watching his eyes as they glanced over towards the machine. He detected fear in them, a brief micro-expression of fear that lasted less than a second but was there, nonetheless. It then dawned on him, in that brief moment, how intimidating his contraption must've looked to someone who wasn't familiar with it. The spiralling shafts, chrome rods, copper coils, and digital displays resembled something from a B-grade sci-fi movie, its entire image screaming out: *danger.*

'Look, I can prove to you that it's safe, and that it works,' said Dillon, suddenly seeing a way out of this. 'The next disaster date that's due to happen is a twelve-car pile-up on the main highway going through District 6. It'll happen in two days' time, and you can watch it with your own eyes. I can tell you a perfect place to watch it from.'

The huge bruiser of a man grinned.

'You're lucky, do you know that? You've caught me at a time when I could use a device like this. People seem to think they can mess with me lately, my shit list keeps on growing, but...I'm not doing any more time. I'm sick of prison food.' He scratched his square chin in contemplation. 'I think this might be the answer to my problems.'

'Yes, and it works! I give you my word on that.'

A horrible silence ensued as the big man considered the situation, the seconds moving along like hours.

'Okay, here's the deal,' he said, finally. 'We're going to watch out for this car accident that you say is going to happen. And, in the meantime, we're taking this machine with us. If this date of yours turns out to be genuine, we'll know that the thing's real and safe to use. And, if that's the case, you won't be seeing any of us again.'

The big man then changed tact, growing sterner, and Dillon watched him crouch down to get level with him, holding out his driving licence so that the name and address was staring him in the face.

'But if this accident doesn't happen, if it turns out that you're messing us around, we'll be paying you a home visit.'

Dillon's face was a picture of fear, but inside he was thinking, *You're not the only one who knows home addresses, pal.*

Dillon watched helplessly as his precious contraption was heaved and scraped outside to a waiting van. Every scratch and dent that was put into it made him wince as though the damage was being inflicted on his own body, but he controlled himself and maintained his composure with the belief that his devious plan might just work.

Once the heavy lifting was done and the machine was secured in the back of the vehicle, Dillon was forced to produce three things: the details of the aforementioned disaster date, the ideal location from which they could all view it from, and some instructions about how to use his machine.

The big man kept to his word, and once the details had been exchanged, they all disappeared and left him alone. He felt shaken up after the surprise encounter, and his back ached after being thrown down on the floor, but even so, a tinge of macabre excitement welled up within him. Sitting alone in the silence of his lockup, with an empty space in the corner where his machine used to be, he knew that something interesting was about to happen.

A thick stream of traffic whizzed by down below as the three men watched on with morbid fascination. Any second now, a cluster of cars would come screeching across the lanes, spraying plastic and glass over the highway, triggering a huge traffic collision. This, in turn, would confirm that the machine they had in their possession was the real deal.

Following the advice that they'd been given, they were watching the road from a balcony high up in an adjacent hotel complex, and they all had to admit that it was a great place to view the main drag from. Leaning over the waist-high metal railing, with the motorway stretched out before them, they felt as though they had ringside seats for this catastrophic spectacle, VIP tickets for the lethal destruction.

They all heard it before they saw it. A thundering crash came resonating through the air from somewhere down below, shaking the ground on which they stood. The timing was right on cue, right down to the second, the explosion erupting at the exact time that it was supposed to. There was, however, one major inaccuracy about the disaster date that they'd been given: the location.

By the time they realised what was happening, it was too late. The entire hotel complex was trembling and growing hotter by the second, and they were trapped high up within it. A smoke alarm blurted out a piercing wail from somewhere behind them, overlaid by the sound of doors slamming and screaming guests running for the stairs.

Then came the smoke and flames.

A furnace-like temperature rose up from the heart of the building in a simmering wave, turning every hallway, room and suite into a soot-filled oven chamber.

Trapped on the balcony, coughing and spluttering, their clothing and skin melting under the embers, the last thing the three men saw before they perished was a group of people shouting and waving at them from the rooftop of an adjacent building, scrambling around with phones pressed to their ears.

The occupants of the rooftop bar on the other side of the road were fretting around in a panic. A horrific scene was unfolding before them, worse than anything they'd ever seen, causing several of them to break down in tears and turn away. Amongst this chaos and despair, however, this crying and anguish, a lone, solitary figure sat calmly in one of the plastic sun-chairs—a wry grin spread across his face.

The plan had worked, the men were dead, and now there was only one more thing to do: retrieve his machine. He knew where to look for it, too. Following Jack a few weeks ago had turned out to be a very good idea, after all. He'd jotted down several addresses as he'd tailed the man doing his rounds, driving past houses and campsites where members of the dreaded family lived, and it was a safe bet that Dillon's machine had been taken to one of these locations.

Rising from the sun-chair, turning away from the rectangular fireball on the other side of the motorway, he made his way to the stairs.

It was time to get his machine.

MORE CHILLS FROM VELOX BOOKS

MORE CHILLS FROM VELOX BOOKS